AN AMISH TEST

The Testing of Ryan and Mattie

Juliet Rohmer

Amish & Christian Romance

Amish and Christian Romance
An Imprint of Ordinary Matters Publishing
www.AmishChristianRomance.com

Book Layout © 2014 BookDesignTemplates.com

An Amish Test / Juliet Rohmer. -- 1st ed. United States of America (Oct 2015)
ISBN-13: 978-1-941303-19-1
ISBN-10: 1941303196

Amish & Christian Romance
PO Box 430577
Houston, Texas 77043
www.AmishChristianRomance.com

Praise for AN AMISH DECISION

"*Lots of Amish adventure here. Just when you think you have it figured out, the author throws in another curve. Love the characters, especially Mattie. Although this is the first part of a series, it doesn't leave you on an annoying cliffhanger. . . . .*

This one's a keeper amidst a sea of Amish books that are maybes and just no's I've read in Amish Romance." ~ Theresa Lepiane, Amazon reviewer

"*One of the best Amish based books I have read. Down to earth and honest in emotion. A must read!*" ~ Devycat, Amazon reviewer

"*I loved this story! Couldn't put it down. I read the first one in the series, and it was enjoyable to read in this story how the two characters meet up again, and what transpired after so many years. Very good read.*" ~ Janis Ellwood, Amazon reviewer

Amish Romance by Juliet Rohmer

Visit and Like Juliet Rohmer's Facebook Fan Page:
Amish Romance Christian Inspirational Romance-Juliet Rohmer

A FREE Amish Romance for You!
For a limited time, you can get a free copy of the next Amish Rumspringa Romance. Sign up:

AmishChristianRomance.com

AN AMISH TEST

THE TESTING OF RYAN AND MATTIE

It's been fifteen years since Matilda King's Rumspringa when she returned to her community to fully embrace the Amish life and married Samuel King. Now she's a widow with all the troubles that brings for a widowed Amish woman with four children and a farm. She's certainly not prepared for an old Englischer flame to step back into her life, let alone join her community.

More disruption follows as Matilda realizes she must make a major life-changing decision and wonders what impact will that have not only on her life but on those around her? She has, after all, been keeping a deep secret all this time.

Rejoicing in hope, patient in tribulation;
continuing instant in prayer....

—ROMANS 12:12 (KJV 1900)

CONTENTS

FOREWARD

I've had a growing interest in Amish romantic fiction for some time. Like many, I am drawn to the idea of a simpler, less chaotic life; a life where devotion to God is the norm and expressed in everyday life. It was inevitable, I guess, that my creative world would become peopled with Amish characters, pastoral landscapes, and a community culture.

To me, these are not simple romantic stories of relationships on the road to happily ever after. The characters are real people with real struggles as they work their way in the world not only toward one another, but also toward the promised land. They may be called Plain people but they are anything but plain.

My love for Matilda King and Ryan Myers and their story continues to grow over the course of *AN AMISH TEST*. It is my hope that you have become equally as fond of Mattie and Ryan and their story of hope as they continue to discover God's will for their lives. As Mattie so often says, "God has a plan."

Happy Reading!

Juliet Rohmer
September 15, 2015

THE TESTING OF RYAN AND MATTIE

CHAPTER ONE

March crashed down upon the San Luis Valley like a rogue wave of unusually warm air. Hopeful buds appeared on bare tree branches, and tender vegetation stirred to life. Columbines sprouted upwards from the damp earth, their vibrant colors peeking out cautiously in the direction of the sun.

Matilda King wiped a hand along the smooth plane of her forehead. She squinted against the bright sunlight from where she stood on the front porch and looked in the direction of the Sangre De Cristo Mountain range. Snow still clung to the mountain sides and even in the fields directly below them. She took a brief moment from cleaning the *haus* of dirt and dust to pray to *Gott* that the warm weather would continue, but she couldn't shake that feeling of dread that blossomed in the center of her chest.

Warm weather in early spring promised two things: chilly temperatures that returned in April and lasted to the beginning of June, or a drought. Matilda prayed that neither occurred. Five springs ago, she remembered vividly how Samuel had spent the night covering the garden with potato sacks but the late snow in early June had won. They replanted and prayed for a warm fall. That summer had been short, dry, and cooler than normal. She'd never forget the distressed look on Samuel's face as he took in the small piles of their harvest, but it didn't last.

Her Samuel always had a backup plan. He traded several hours of fixing buggies for more vegetables and used the Farmers Market to purchase meat to supply them through the harsh winter.

Matilda felt her stomach tighten in longing. She would give anything to have Samuel and his backup plans once again, especially now that she could be facing yet another hard planting season.

"*Ach!*"

The sound of Isaac's voice crying in surprise drew Matilda's attention back to where her *kinner* were currently taking advantage of the strange heat at the beginning of March. She assessed the situation and smiled.

"Mama!" Isaac cried, pointing a pale finger at Rosella. "She sprayed water at me."

A large wet stain covered the front of Isaac's button shirt. Rosella blinked innocently with the hose on the muddy ground alongside her. "I didn't do anything. Isaac got himself wet."

"I did not!" He glared at Rosella. "You sprayed me with water. Now, my shirt is all wet."

"Don't be such a *bobli.*"

Matilda stepped off the front porch to intervene before a fight could ensue. Her *kinner* loved one another, but being cooped up all winter in the *haus* had worn on everyone's nerves. She approached Isaac and placed a gentle hand on his head and felt the heat of the sun in the silky strands of hair.

"Go inside and change. I don't want you to catch a cold while working in a damp shirt."

"But it's warm out," he protested, now happy to forget his wet shirt.

"Inside, now."

At the firmness of her tone, Isaac's shoulders dropped. He shot Rosella one last glowering glare before disappearing into the *haus*. Meanwhile, Matthew looked first at Matilda, then at Rosella. Matilda tried not to smile when Mathew, clearly sensing the tension building between Rosella and his mother, grabbed a watering pail and beat a hasty retreat to the garden.

Rosella stared at the ground in an obvious attempt to avoid her mother's gaze. Over the past few months, Matilda had noticed a change in Rosella's behavior. While normally well-behaved (besides occasional bouts of sassiness), her daughter's mood seemed to have darkened. Rosella often withdrew into silent thoughts and replied to her mother's inquires in a strained voice. Her *bruders* seemed to be the main target of her changing moods, and Matilda wondered what sort of confrontation was going on between them.

Rosella was the first to speak. "Aren't you going to say something?" she asked, her voice flat and surly.

"I was hoping you would tell me what was going on," Matilda replied and leveled a pointed glance at her when Rosella looked up. "Particularly, what's going on with you?"

Those all too familiar sapphire eyes shifted away, veiling whatever turbulent emotions were at play within her daughter. Matilda sighed. It was a subtle withdrawal. She had always been close to Rosella, but she knew eventually her daughter would exhibit some of this behavior. Rosella might be Amish through and through, but she had also reached her teenage years.

Matilda took a deep breath and tried a different approach. She took a step towards Rosella, while offering a smile of peace. "Whatever it is, Rosella, you can tell me. I promise not to get mad if that is what worries you."

"That isn't what I worry about."

Another wall. A headache started to pound in the back of Matilda's head. She refused to show any sign of inward aggravation at her daughter's distant behavior.

"Well?" she said, when Rosella didn't continue. "What's going on?"

Rosella twisted her hands in the apron tied tightly around her trim waist as she chewed on her bottom lip. Matilda remained quiet as she met her daughter's searching look. A warm breeze played with an errant strand of honey blonde hair that escaped the pins of her daughter's *kapp*.

"You promise to not get mad or defensive over it?"

"*Ja*," Matilda said, agreeing quickly and happy to see a break in the wall, "I promise. Whatever it is, I promise to be open."

"Okay. I—"

The distant crunch of horse hooves on gravel alerted both of them that someone was coming down their road. Matilda noticed how Rosella glanced over her shoulder and tensed when she caught sight of the driver sitting in the buggy seat.

"I'm going inside," she muttered, kicking the hose out of the way. "I'm not feeling *gut*."

"Rosella—"

Her oldest gave no indication of hearing her plea. Instead, Rosella stomped up the front porch steps and slammed the door behind her. Matilda felt the pounding headache spread and rubbed her temples with the pads of her fingers as she turned to look up at the driver of the buggy.

Golden strands of hair sparkled in the warm sunlight and appeared to glow with more brightness than usual. Matilda couldn't stop herself as she took in the chiseled facial features and the strong hands grasping the leather reigns in such a sure way. Dressed in traditional Amish clothes, Ryan Myers remained unbearably handsome to look upon from his strong physique to his clean-shaven jaw; a sign of his marriage status.

"Morning," he said, flashing a grin that showed off his white teeth. "I was just taking this buggy for a spin to check out my work."

"So you came by my *haus*?" she said dryly.

Her strained question seemed to dampen his cheerful mood. He would be in a *gut* mood Matilda thought with a small inward smile. Adjusting to the Amish way of life had not been exactly easy for Ryan since the start of his testing period in January. The harsh winter elements didn't help him much when he had to chop wood outside in the middle of a frigid night or learn how to keep a fire going all night in the wood stove.

"How do you people live without electricity?" Ryan complained one afternoon, nursing a cold and a bad mood with a cup of chamomile tea. "I mean, the wood stove is great and all, but having to put wood in the thing every two hours is disrupting my sleep schedule. I might as well have a newborn baby if this is how it will be."

"I'll show you how to keep a fire going all night," Matilda volunteered, hoping to assure him. If *Gott* wanted her to help him along with his journey, she could surely show him the trick Samuel had shown her when it came to keeping the house warm at night.

She tried to keep her distance, though, and only offered help when needed. They were, after all, just friends. The statement felt irritatingly overused by now from how frequently Matilda repeated it to neighbors, friends, and even to her family. Ryan naturally glued himself to Matilda since joining the community for his testing period, and it was a bit unnerving sometimes to know that he trusted her that much. He had taken up a job in the same buggy shop Samuel used to work in and lived with their Bishop's older *bruder* who needed the help around the farm and *haus*. Ryan made it a point to stop by the bakery every lunch break to talk with Matilda, and to run through the Pennsylvania Dutch she was teaching him.

"I'm sorry?" Ryan posed it as a question, but a confused frown settled in his brow. "Did I break some sort of rule again by coming by the house? I seem to do that a lot more frequently now."

Matilda bit her tongue to keep her thoughts to herself. The first few months had been fine what with Ryan getting used to putting aside the luxuries of an English lifestyle. He seemed to be more at peace than when he first arrived in their community. Although he was willing and eager to learn every aspect of their lifestyle, Matilda's skepticism still continued to grow every day. She caught his confused frowns at church as he tried to understand the fast flowing sermons and saw a sadness that sometimes occupied his eyes when no one was watching.

Tiny breaks splintered Ryan's magnetic personality, but apparently she was the only one who noticed. The rest of the community was either smitten by his charming tongue on the rare occasions when he would talk, or they had their doubts that someone like him could truly live for *Gott*.

Matilda was also not unaware of the undercurrent of tension that pulled at them since what had been said back in January when Ryan first embraced their lifestyle and embarked on this year of testing. She truly believed *Gott* had a plan for both of them and Ryan insisted that he felt the same way. She prayed every day, seeking *Gott's* advice, and searching for answers on the direction of their relationship. Sure, there were the flirtatious comments that slipped from Ryan's tongue that had Matilda's blood quickening, but she was quick to calm herself and refrain from temptation through prayer and her strength in *Gott*. She knew any growing attachment toward Ryan would allow those old feelings to be stirred and would put her directly on the path for trouble.

Matilda wiped her sweaty palms on the front of her apron and absently smoothed a few wrinkles from her blue dress before answering Ryan's question. She still felt a bit odd wearing colors even though the period of wearing mourning clothes had finally ended. For her, the change was only on the physical level. Within her heart she still missed and mourned Samuel.

"You can't just show up to my *haus*." she said, trying to keep the exasperation out of her voice. "I have my *kinner* here, and I already have to keep explaining to the community that we are just friends. It does not look *gut* when you show up without a reason."

The rebuke went either unnoticed or Ryan was simply unperturbed by the rumors swirling around. He glanced over at the nearest neighboring farm, and then looked back at Matilda with a scoff.

"There's no one around to talk about us." he said. "Why do you listen to all that talk anyway? I don't listen or give a second thought to how the community thinks I won't even make it."

Ryan dropped the reigns and stretched his long arms above him. The casual gesture made Matilda squirm. She kept one eye trained to look out for her *kinner* who were already confused as to why Ryan made frequent visits. Her *kinner* seemed wary of him and his intentions, as was she.

"Is there something that you need, Ryan? I have a lot to do around the *haus*."

"You're doing work on a Saturday? It's the weekend."

"You have been here for how many months, Ryan? You know that we work on Saturdays and rest on Sundays."

Ryan shrugged and gave her one of his expansive smiles. "I still propose that everyone should have the weekend off. Maybe I'll suggest it to the Bishop tomorrow morning."

Matilda tried to keep a lid on her irritation as it bubbled dangerously over. Little comments like those that he uttered more frequently lately only added to her doubts about Ryan's commitment to *Gott* and the *Ordnung*. All the more reason to put distance between them.

When she didn't respond, Ryan held up his hands in surrender. "Only kidding, Mattie," he said, "I was just making a joke."

"Don't call me—"

"Mattie. I got it," he said, gathering the reins again and keeping a cool expression. "I'll let you be so you can stay in a grumpy mood."

Matilda stared up at him, trying to read his emotions. He met her gaze evenly before flicking the reigns gently and with a cluck of his tongue, gracefully turning the buggy around to head back up the road.

Just like that he left her standing on the front lawn of her *haus*, his antics leaving her torn between irritation and amusement. She glanced over her shoulder towards the garden, but found Matthew patting the ground to assess how much water the garden needed. The flutter of curtains upstairs drew her attention and for the briefest second she caught Rosella standing at the window, staring with yet one more scowl toward the vanishing horse and buggy.

It clicked then as to the source of Rosella's moods, and deep down Matilda felt the flutter of fear take flight once again. "*Gott* help me," she said, praying out loud.

Rebecca stood in front of Matilda with arms crossed firmly across her chest and a wooden spatula clutched in one hand. "I heard that Ryan stopped by your *haus* this weekend—again."

A wet chill still clung to the morning air as it swept through the kitchen in a breeze that stirred the bottom of their dresses. The faint smell of a late-night rain filled Matilda's nose as she breathed in to control her temper. Her mother had arched an eyebrow in that annoying way that trumpeted her readiness for an argument.

"Nothing is going on," Matilda said, totally exasperated, "for the hundredth time, *maemm*." Matilda knew she had to have a serious talk with Ryan about his showing up to her *haus* without invitation or reason.

"You expect me or the community to believe that?" Rebecca scoffed loudly. "That man has attached himself to you, and it is not doing your reputation any *gut* having this sort of gossip running around the community like wildfire."

Matilda turned around to face Rebecca and scoffed back at her in return. "You're worried about my reputation? You have made it worse, *maemm*, by talking to people about Ryan and how he is around way too much at the bakery."

"Of course I'm concerned about it. I'm your *maemm*, and I don't want to see you return someone's affections when they are not serious about joining our way of life. He is an Englischer through and through."

The jingle of the bell above the door thankfully stopped the conversation in mid track giving Matilda a needed moment of relief.

Rebecca waved a warning finger. "This conversation isn't over, Matilda."

Her mother hurried to the front of the bakery leaving Matilda alone with her pies. The smell of cocoa powder filled her lungs as she breathed in to squash her temper. With nimble fingers, Matilda skimmed the top of the measuring spoon to assure the right amount of powder was going in. She found the cheerful voices of the Englischers at the front of the bakery coupled with the warm spring breeze coming through the back door a needed distraction from the earlier conversation.

Shoes squeaked on the linoleum floor and a presence breezed behind Matilda in the direction of the stove as she raised her eyes in time to catch Lily's friendly smile before checking on the apple pies they had put together earlier. Her sister's upbeat mood had little to do with working in the bakery. Lily had turned sixteen a few weeks earlier, and last week their *maemm* and *daed* had given Lily permission to leave the community with a group of friends for Rumspringa. The mere thought of Lily on Rumspringa was enough to make Matilda shiver as the image of her sister dressed in English dresses and sipping on beer while chatting with an English boy populated her mind. Her sister's delicate features would undoubtedly attract attention — and boys.

Lily's smile slipped and a concerned frown formed. "You okay, Matilda? You're looking at me funny."

Matilda batted away the memories threatening to surface. She cleared her throat, and tipped the measuring spoon over to add more cocoa to the whoopie pie mixture.

"*Ja*, I'm fine. Are those pies ready?"

"*Nee*. In a few minutes they will be," Lily replied, and crossed her arms across her chest. "I heard *maemm* and you arguing this morning. What was it about this time?"

Matilda's mood soured once again at the question. She picked up a whisk and twirled the dry mixture around with stiff movements. First it was Rosella who pointedly ignored Matilda all weekend other than saying a few words, and then it was her *maemm* asking questions. Before she could answer or elaborate on what had happened, Lily answered for her.

"It was about Ryan again, *ja*?"

"*Ja*." Matilda said and sighed, pausing her movements. "She was asking about our relationship; the one that doesn't even exist."

Lily slowly approached the kitchen island where Matilda stood and placed her hands on the edge. She chewed on her bottom lip for a few seconds before speaking in a cautious voice. "Don't get mad when I say this, but can you honestly blame us for wondering what is going on? You two are seen together constantly at church after the sermons, he's here during lunch breaks, and he hasn't really interacted with anyone else besides you and a few others."

"I know all that, but we're just friends." Even to Matilda, the statement felt thick and rough coming out of her mouth. She swallowed it down, and knew from the dubious look Lily sent her that she did not believe one word. Matilda tried again. "He needs someone to help him through this period in his life, and I want to help him."

The admission slipped out and dangled in the space between them. Matilda felt the sides of her neck flare up, and immediately dropped her gaze to the abandoned bowl. Despite her hesitance and fears, she could not turn away from Ryan. Her compassion for him had grown on its own, and perhaps that troubled her more than anything else. It definitely made it hard to distance herself from Ryan even though logic urged her to do so.

Lily gave her a soft smile. "You've always been so compassionate. *Maemm* told me how you used to bring home stray kittens and feed them so they wouldn't starve to death."

"Anybody would do that," Matilda said, uncomfortable hearing her sister's words.

"Maybe, but don't you see it? Everyone knows there is something going on between you two, and has been since Ryan arrived here. You can't be that blind to it."

"There's nothing going on."

At Matilda's words, Lily sighed. She picked up a towel, and folded it into a neat square before placing it back on the kitchen island. "I don't think you believe that. There is something there; you just don't want to admit it."

"Lily, I don't want to talk about this," Matilda said, refusing to meet Lily's gaze.

Lily pressed on. "I'm all for Ryan. I think he's a *gut* man, and you are different around him. Different in a *gut* way that I've never seen before."

Tears obscured Matilda's vision of the bowl and counter top. She sucked in a watery breath, fighting the emotions that were rising like a tsunami within her. She dropped the whisk in the bowl and dodged towards the back door.

"Matilda? I'm sorry—"

Matilda shut the door behind her before Lily could say anything else or chase after her. The blue skies above were clear of clouds, and still a dark hue of blue from the winter seasons. She tilted her head back to allow the warm sunlight to dry the wetness coating her cheeks and started down the sidewalk to clear her mind.

Anger coursed through her. Anger towards Ryan, towards her family, towards her community churned within her and burned painfully in the middle of her chest. Why had *Gott* brought Ryan back? What sort of test was this? The community's eyes were fixed upon them, and Matilda was desperate to get out of the spotlight while Ryan ignored any skepticism thrown in his direction.

You are different around him. Different in a gut way that I've never seen before.

Oh, Samuel. Matilda called out to him. More than anything she wished for him to be there with her right now, enveloping her in that big reassuring hug. What would he think hearing Lily's words?

Matilda paused in front of an empty playground with rusted equipment and sat on a bench to watch the cars drive by. She curled her fingers around the metal that was warmed from the sun. When she closed her eyes, her mother popped into mind and their earlier conversation.

A bird chirping nearby drew her back and she slumped backwards against the bench. She had to form some plan that would distance herself from Ryan. Her mind whirled but only ended up in failed attempts. In the end, she knew there was one thing she needed to do.

She had to talk to Rosella.

CHAPTER TWO

A hot breeze tickled the back of Matilda's neck, playing the wispy strands of her hair there. She closed her eyes at the gentle caress, and soaked in the sound of her community's voices singing in unison. Church never failed to bring her peace. They fell into a prayer, and Matilda prayed for strength. She prayed even harder for guidance to sort through the mess of emotions within her. No matter how hard she tried to process them, she ended up in the same place as before. Confused. Angry. Terrified.

Gott, please help me. Help me through this test and to understand its purpose.

The faint brush of Rosella's arm against hers drew Matilda back from her prayers. She glanced over at her daughter sitting stiffly on the bench next to her and resisted the urge to reach out and grab her hand. Their exchanges were still curt and brief. With the warm weather and increase in business at the bakery, Matilda found little time to sit Rosella down for a talk over what was troubling her.

Goosebumps spread across Matilda's shoulders when she became aware of someone's gaze. She swallowed thickly, her fingers curled tightly around the *Ausband*. She resisted the urge to turn her head and look in Ryan's direction. Not when their community surrounded them and, she knew, was watching their every exchange.

The last hymn was sung slowly before happy chatter filled the barn they were currently seated in. Everyone moved in a steady stream toward the late morning sunshine and to set up the tables for their usual potluck of food. Matilda kept her hands on the back of Matthew and Isaac's necks as she led them outside. She turned to address Rosella, but found her already with a group of friends a few feet away. Matilda's heart gave a sharp twang of longing for their close relationship again, for those times when Rosella would let her brush her hair before pinning on her *kapp*.

"Still fighting?" Rebecca appeared suddenly at Matilda's side, smiling fondly down at Matthew and Isaac.

"We're not fighting." Once again her mother seemed to see into her heart. True, there had been no harsh words exchanged, or any arguments for that matter, with Rosella. Only brief conversations, and a growing distance, between them. "I don't know what's going on exactly."

"Mama." Matthew started suddenly and pointed eagerly to the *kinner* running around in the field behind the barn. "Can we go play? Please?"

"*Ja*, but you have to come back to eat," Matilda said, calling after them as they sprinted happily towards the hay field.

At that moment, Ryan emerged from the barn behind them. Their hands brushed in passing, and a heat filled the center of Matilda's cheeks at the contact. She withdrew her hand, unsure if it were intentional, or accidental, and immediately dropped her gaze to the ground to avoid making eye contact.

Rebecca cut a pointed glance at Matilda as Ryan strode away towards the table that was now filled with food. "Are you sure you don't know? Because it's obvious to everyone around you what's bothering Rosella."

Matilda acknowledged her mother's words. "All right, *maemm*. I have an idea of what's bothering her. I'm just trying to figure out a way to talk to her about," she said and couldn't stop a deep sigh.

"What is there to talk about? You know what it is bothering her, and yet you aren't willing to address it. You haven't addressed it in the past few months."

Matilda turned to look out at the still snow-clad mountains and to regroup her thoughts. Dark clouds twisted around the white peaks, and thunder boomed distantly. What little peace that had built within Matilda during church dissipated with what hung between herself and Rebecca.

"Because there isn't anything to talk about." Matilda answered tightly. She turned to look at Rebecca with pleading eyes. "Please, *maemm*. I don't wish to talk about this anymore. Not at church."

Matilda felt the intensity of her mother's gaze lessen before she finally heard a quiet, "Okay."

Matilda felt as though she could breathe again.

"Let's enjoy Fellowship with our community," Rebecca said and left Matilda to join their community and blended easily into the sea of *kapps*.

Matilda followed in her *maemm's* steps. After checking her *kinner* had plates of food, Matilda retreated to a large oak tree to take advantage of the shade. Her cheeks felt flushed and sweaty from an already hot morning. She looked out and relaxed as she saw that she could easily keep an eye on Isaac and Matthew as they played down in the field.

"Can I sit here with you?"

Matilda squeaked in surprise at the sound of Ryan's voice directly behind her and nearly choked on a bite of cottage cheese salad. She turned around to look upwards, still coughing rather unattractively.

"Don't sneak up on me like that!"

Ryan frowned and shoved both hands into the pockets of his trousers. "I wasn't sneaking up on you, and I'm sorry that I startled you. Can I sit here with you?" he repeated.

She fiddled with edges of her plate as she debated on telling him no, but found herself giving in when he gave her a pleading look. With a sigh, she motioned for him to sit. He folded his long legs in front of him and wrapped his arms loosely around his bent knees.

"Beautiful day out," he commented, looking at the sky. "I don't think I've ever known a spring to be this warm."

Several pairs of eyes were fixated on them sitting alone at the oak tree, but it was her *maemm's* threatening to burn holes into hers that stood out against the curious stares of Martha and the other *fraas* watching them. They all whispered together as they hovered about the tables, loading plates of food for their *mansleit* and *kinner*. Matilda's skin prickled under the sensation, and she ducked her head to focus on her plate of food instead.

"*Ja,* beautiful for now."

"For now?"

"Whenever there is an early spring, it is usually bad news for us in late spring." Matilda explained.

"How will it be bad for us in late spring? We get an early start to planting season. Wouldn't that mean a bigger harvest?"

Matilda laughed softly under her breath and absently picked at her plate of food. "We can only pray. You've never been here for an early spring to see what can happen."

"Enlighten me then."

She frowned at his exasperated tone. Ryan sat next to her, his body tight and tense, his hands twisting nervously in front of his legs. She could see his jaw clenching and unclenching before turning his head to meet her gaze.

"What?" He questioned, annoyance glittering faintly in those sapphire depths that could easily drown her.

"Why are you so angry?"

"I'm not angry. Annoyed, maybe, but not angry."

Matilda felt her curiosity piqued. Yes, she wanted to distance herself from him, and yet she was still a friend and a spiritual advisor to help whenever he was in need. Despite the conflicted feelings currently occupying the recesses of her heart, she did feel a thread of responsibility for his well being. If *Gott* intended for her to help Ryan transition over, to accept the *Ordnung*, and to commit himself to their lifestyle, she would not turn her head.

She just needed to guard her heart.

Matilda prayed for *Gott's* guidance before she spoke. "Ryan, what's going on for you to be annoyed? You're usually in a *gut* mood most of the time."

He let out a deep sigh and reached up to push off the black hat the men wore for church and smoothed a hand over the honey blonde strands of his head. At the movement, the crisp white shirt pulled tautly against his strong shoulder. The smell of spice and whatever soap he had used permeated Matilda's senses, and she found herself inhaling deeply without thinking.

"I think it has finally hit me," he said, as he turned even more to look at her. His foot brushed against the side of her leg, and she quickly moved it to avoid further contact. "The first few months here have been a pleasant break from all the noise and clutter that had been my life. You have no idea how great it's been to live simply without having to worry about money or making tight deadlines. Just to be close to *Gott*...."

Matilda heard a sadness in his voice and waited as her heart pumped hard. She had an idea of where Ryan was going with the conversation. They had talked about his frustrations over adjusting to the culture and missing his sister Olivia. It was one of the main reasons why she remained skeptical about Ryan's ability to adjust to the Amish life. It was also why she refused to admit any sort of feelings to him to anyone or to herself.

"I just miss Olivia, and I wonder what's going on with my business. I wonder how things are out there. I feel a bit cut off from the world, and it's driving me crazy little by little."

She saw his despair as he dragged his hands down the side of his chiseled face as he released another sigh. Matilda chewed on her bottom lip. Even now, after all these years, she recalled the constant noise in the city. She had been amazed that anyone was able to sleep at night from all the strange man-made sounds. She had been utterly relieved to come back to her quiet community and to listen to the quiet chirp of crickets rather than the busy blare of sirens going off in the distance.

She felt him shift and relax a little after his admission before he went on, his voice quieter. "It doesn't make sense, I know. It's just how I feel at times."

While Matilda could never completely understand what Ryan was going through, she did identify with the feelings of isolation and despair. These were the times she felt *Gott* wanted her to help counsel him, to help him through the sadness and hardship he was currently facing. She briefly closed her eyes to pray, and then picked her words carefully.

"I know this time is hard for you. Our lifestyle is not easy, especially if you have not grown up and lived as one in the community. It's an adjustment living the way we do. But you are not the first to want to make the change; in time, you'll become more and more accustomed to our way of life and to what *Gott* wants from you."

If you stay.

She wanted to say those last words, but kept them to herself. It was better to keep her doubts quiet.

Ryan leaned back against the tree and she saw him shed a layer of anxiety as he spoke. "I hope you're right, Mattie. I really hope you're right."

"You'll see. *Gott* wouldn't have brought you here and not given you guidance. He has a plan. Look at His creation around us." Matilda swept a hand in the direction of the Sangre de Cristo Mountains where white peaks stood starkly against the powder blue sky that was free from clouds. "You can't see this in Denver with all those metal buildings in the way. Listen to the quiet. Sometimes it becomes so silent that you can almost hear *Gott* speak with you in the breeze. Oh, Ryan, there isn't a day that I don't thank *Gott* for giving all this to me. Give it time, and know I'm here if you need me."

"Wow."

Matilda had been so caught up in *Gott* and His creation that she stood aside as the words tumbled out of her. The expansive feeling that had taken over suddenly fled as she realized how intense she'd become.

"Mattie, I would've sworn you were a poet there instead of an Amish woman."

Her smile froze in its spot when Ryan chuckled, a deep noise from within the caverns of his chest. In that instant she was sixteen years old again, her heart palpitating with fluttery nerves at the intoxicating sound. They lapsed back into a companionable silence while watching their community laugh together. For that one moment, they were just content to be next to one another.

Monday, Matilda unhitched a whinnying Pepper from the buggy, and turned him loose to happily graze in the field behind the bakery. A quiet and rather sullen looking Rosella stood besides the buggy as she waited for Matilda to return from the field.

"Why couldn't I stay home today?" Rosella asked.

Matilda held an exasperated sigh in check. She grabbed both their lunch pails from the buggy and pointed to the back door of the bakery. "You're not talking yourself out of this, Rosella. With the fabric store closed today, we could use your help baking."

With schooling finished, Rosella begged Matilda to let her work with her best friend, Lucy at her *maemm's* fabric store on the main street. While she was a good baker like all Amish tended to be, her daughter preferred other things like sewing. Matilda had relented with the agreement that Rosella would help out at the bakery whenever she could, but Matilda took the distance to heart. She knew that Rosella would eventually pull away to start her own family and life within the community, but it seemed to be happening too fast.

Gravel crunched underneath their sneakered feet as they crossed the small parking lot to the propped open door. Although it was still early, a hot air had already settled down in the valley and promised another hot afternoon. For Matilda, that meant a miserable day in front of the oven that was fueled by chopped wood below, while having to deal with another of Rosella's recent spells of moodiness.

The second they entered the small kitchen at the back of the bakery, Rosella busied herself by carefully slicing crust to make a lattice for an apple pie. She kept her head bowed as she concentrated on the task and pointedly ignored any attempt to have further conversation.

Matilda busied herself with tasks that kept her moving from the back baking area to the front, which meant she had to deal with both her mother and her daughter. One kept watching her while the other did anything but.

"I see that you're still fighting," Rebecca finally said.

Matilda set the tray of whoopie pies in the display case and gently shut the glass sliding door. She turned to give her *maemm* an exasperated glare in the hopes she'd take the hint but knew her *maemm* wouldn't let the frosty silence continue.

"We aren't fighting about anything. She's just upset with some things that she has probably heard."

She watched as her *maemm* pursed her lips and fought the urge to make some sort of response. Instead, Rebecca busied herself around the cash register, tidying up the area.

Much to Matilda's annoyance and fear, she knew there were still whispers going about the community, talk her *maemm* was bound to hear. Although gossip was frowned upon, it happened and some people always gave in to their curiosity. Matilda thought about what she had heard and seen and ticked off several incidents. Martha had questioned her several times over her and Ryan's relationship. She also had overheard Betty asking Rosella at church one Sunday afternoon if the rumors of her mother and Ryan courting were true. None of the rumors were malicious, simply idle talk about their newest member of the community who only seemed to talk with Matilda. She knew the community looked with skepticism on Ryan's attempt to live among them, and she recognized that they had *gut* reason. Ryan had a rather charming tongue and a foreword personality that clashed with the Amish more humble nature. His past of being a successful and smooth-talking business man wasn't a secret, and it certainly didn't help that his sometimes over-friendly behavior that could easily be mistaken as flirtatiousness.

Matilda knew of several of the younger women in the community who had yet to be married who had mistaken Ryan's engaging ways. She heard their excited chatter sometimes during the day when they passed by the bakery. She didn't blame them; after all, she'd succumbed to that her charm herself when young. Nor was she that alarmed by the flicker of jealousy inside her heart. She held firm to the notion that she and Ryan had no chance of a romantic relationship, especially during the time of his testing and certainly not until he was a part of the church. What happened after that she would not entertain.

Lost in her own thoughts, Matilda didn't realize Rebecca had stopped with her busywork and had turned her attention toward her daughter. She braced herself for yet another reprimand and was shocked to see a gentleness take over her *maemm's* face as she simply said, "Then talk to her, Matilda. Talk to your daughter."

Then Rebecca shooed her from behind the counter to the hot kitchen and shut the door firmly behind her. Matilda surveyed the kitchen and inhaled the smell of freshly baked apple pie as Rosella pulled a bubbling pie from the oven.

Steeling herself, she approached her daughter. "That looks *gut*," she said. "The crust is a perfect golden color and smells *wunderbar*."

She was rewarded by a simple *"Danka."*

Rosella set the pie on a cooling rack before slipping off her oven mitts and tossing them onto the counter. She presented Matilda her back by gathering a couple of bowls to wash in the sink. Flour dusted the sleeves of her gray dress, and when the sunlight from the window above the sink landed on the curve of her cheek, granules of sugar sparkled on her sharp cheekbones. Meanwhile, soap bubbles covered Rosella's wrists as she made quick work of the dirty bowls.

Matilda had no choice but to address her daughter's back. "Rosella, what is going on with you?"

Rosella gave her the expected defensive reply. "Nothing."

Matilda tried again. "I don't believe you. Why don't we sit outside and talk while the other pies bake? We have time."

"I don't want to talk about it."

Matilda fought back an angry retort but realized moving Rosella was going to be a much more difficult task than expected. "Then as your *maemm* I'm telling you that you don't have a choice. Put the pies in the oven, and let's go outside for a moment."

At Matilda's more strident tone, Rosella finally looked over her shoulder only to give her that same scowl. Matilda stared back nonplussed by the rebellious streak that Rosella was currently fighting through. She didn't remember acting so, so stubborn and difficult with her own *maemm*. Of course, Rebecca probably wouldn't have allowed things to get that far. Matilda fought the urge to unleash a barrage of words upon her daughter's head and opted for a quiet, waiting stare.

After several rather long minutes, Rosella offered a short reply. "Fine."

Wiping her hands on a dish towel, Rosella placed the other pies in the oven and double checked the wood beneath before following Matilda outside. The air felt cooler compared to the hot air inside the kitchen and greeted them with the comfortable scent of pine. Perhaps they were in need of a trip up to the mountains, Matilda thought absently. They had made those short getaways several times with Samuel whenever they reached an impasse and couldn't find a solution. He had always believed that *Gott* could reach them through the whisper of the wind up there, and their family would spend hours praying together on a barn blanket while enjoying whatever lunch Matilda packed. Sometimes their *kinner* would slip off their shoes and splash alongside in a bubbling creek.

Matilda smiled inwardly at the warm memories of taking the buggy up the winding mountain roads and praying under the canopy of green foliage within reach of a creek trickling nearby. Being surrounded by *Gott's* creations did wonders for the soul. Whatever problems that plagued them then were gone under the light of *Gott* coming through the leafy tree tops.

Rosella moodily scuffed the bottom of her sneaker on the gravel and held her crossed her arms tightly against her chest. "What do you want to talk about?"

Matilda prayed for patience. She knew her daughter well and exchanging heated words would do neither one of them any good. She prayed even harder for strength as she tried to consider all that might be bothering Rosella.

"I know that you have probably heard some things going around the community about my relationship with Ryan."

"Relationship?" Rosella's eyes nearly bugged out. "You're courting him, *maemm?* Everyone was right! You're—"

"Hold on," Matilda cut in, alarmed by the outburst of words. "That was the wrong word to use. We aren't in any sort of relationship, Rosella. We are just friends. We can't even court in the first place."

Rosella looked partially relieved, but her skepticism still painted her tanned face. No matter what season *Gott* graced them with, Matilda thought, her daughter's skin always remained the same golden hue.

"Then why hasn't he made any friends with anyone else?"

Matilda resisted a sigh. "I don't know. He's having a hard time adjusting to our faith and to our lifestyle. An Englischer has a hard time letting go of their life and their world, especially when it's all they've known."

"I understand that, but why is he such close friends with you, and you only?"

Matilda felt her face warm and fanned herself absently. She couldn't' help but wonder when her daughter had become so observant. Then again, Rosella always had a sharp eye for certain details. She often caught Rosella observing the people around her before she would step forward and speak. Perhaps she shouldn't be all that surprised.

Matilda sought to put her daughter off. "That's a complicated question to answer."

"*Nee.* It's not. It's rather simple."

Nothing about this is simple, Matilda thought. "It's not simple, Rosella."

"You wanted to talk, *maemm*. I want to know what's going on with you and Ryan. Everyone else seems to think that you two are more than friends or have been at some point."

Matilda felt the cold weight of dread at her daughter's words and felt her stomach twist with a sharp cramp. "Who has been telling you these things?"

Rosella shrugged. "No one specifically. Betty mentioned to me that she overheard her *daed* telling the Bishop that he is concerned about Ryan's true intentions towards you, as well as his desire to join the church."

Matilda closed her eyes briefly in what felt like non-stop exasperation. While her friendship with Eli had grown increasingly strained since Ryan's arrival, Eli's daughter and Rosella's friendship only grew. The two were approaching Rumspringa together, and both shared grief over losing a parent. She should've known that Betty would've heard Eli voice his displeasure over Ryan but she never thought he'd go to the Bishop. Their interactions over the past few months were incredibly awkward and filled with tension. While Eli honored her decision to remain friends, he clearly desired and still expected her to return his affections. She should have done more to discourage his frequent stops at the bakery and pointed attempts at conversation after church. *How had this become such a tangled mess, Gott?*

"*Maemm?* Are you okay? You look pale."

She blinked back to where Rosella stood in front of her with a concerned frown. Matilda swallowed and felt the fear lodged in her throat. She couldn't think of a response. Instead she twisted her hands together to keep her nerves at bay and searched for a response that would settle Rosella's question. Her mind remained blank and a slow, creeping fear filled her. What if she told Rosella the truth? Matilda knew, without question, that her daughter would be devastated. Her heart ached as she thought of the heartbreak the truth would inflict on Rosella alone. The wildfire that would then spread throughout the community wouldn't compare to her daughter's pain. Matilda sought refuge in *Gott* and His promises, yet she remained afraid.

"Tell me it isn't true, *maemm*. Tell me that you two haven't been..." Rosella trailed off, unable to say it.

Matilda saw her daughter's cheeks burn bright red. The sunlight bore down on her own *kapp*, but she knew the heat Rosella felt had nothing to do with the sun. Forcing an assuring smile, she confronted her daughter's words "It isn't true. A long time ago we knew each other, when I was younger, and that's all there is to it."

"Are you sure about that, *maemm?* I don't think his intentions towards you involve friendship. I agree with *Grohs-mammi* when she says that there is something else going on between you and him. We've seen the way he looks at you at church. I don't understand why you are trying to hide it from me. You've never hidden anything from me, and now this...."

Rosella airily waved her hand to prove her point.

"I'm not trying to hide anything, Rosella," Matilda said and sought to respond to the unmistakable hurt tone. She reached out to touch her daughter gingerly on the shoulder, but Rosella dodged the attempt and would have none of it.

"*Ja,* you are. I know that you are. You just don't want to admit that you are hiding something. We lost *daed,* and then it was Eli, and now you're hiding secrets."

"Rosella —"

"I have to go back in. The pies will be ready."

Matilda felt the tears slip as she watched Rosella turn away and head for the kitchen. This had been another reason why she had wished Ryan wouldn't come to the community. It was clear that her family would never truly accept him because of their doubts over his commitment to *Gott* and their community, and allowing those carefully contained emotions to develop would cause discourse. She was not willing to lose her *kinner* nor her family at the expense of being with Ryan. Not when she wasn't even confident in him being able to truly devout himself to *Gott* and their Amish life. She prayed that *Gott* would give her strength and the knowledge to deal with her daughter and with Ryan.

Matilda wasn't even sure letting go of Samuel was possible. He still lived within her heart always. She talked to him at night and sometimes in the morning during prayers. Allowing herself to fall in love with a different man felt sinful and against her marriage vows to Samuel.

"Why *Gott,* is this happening?" she whispered, clutching her hands together. "I have asked for forgiveness and followed your word. Why is this happening now?"

The distant boom of thunder reached Matilda's ears as she stared blearily up at the clouds. The storm clouds had gathered again above the mountain peaks, and each boom signaled an approaching storm, one she also felt deep within her heart.

CHAPTER THREE

With the unusual bout of hot air occupying the valley, an increase of business kept the bakery busy with orders and with Englischers trickling in steadily throughout the day. Matilda spent the mornings standing in front of a hot stove, fueling the flames beneath it, and trying not to faint from the heat. Tuesday was no different as she placed a few whoopie pies into the scorching oven.

"Why don't you go to the local grocery store and get more vanilla?" Rebecca said, pressing some money into Matilda's palm "You look as if you need a break."

Matilda knew, from her mother's stare, that her cheeks were flush from the heat and signaling her exhaustion. "Are you sure?" she asked. "There's pies and —"

"Lily and I can handle the pies," Rebecca said and waved her hand as a sign of dismissal. "Besides, we need to take advantage of Lily being here before she goes off on her Rumspringa in a few weeks."

Matilda glanced through the door to where Lily stood behind the cash register with her fingers dancing across the buttons. Rumspringa. The word alone brought Matilda the shivers. How much her life had changed during that brief stretch of time, and how it burdened her with a deep-rooted secret. She prayed that Lily would never make such life altering decisions, even if they felt innocent. *Gott* knew

Matilda had never realized that one night of temptation would lead to the events that followed. She watched Lily, nearly grown up now, handle customers with such confidence. When had her little sister grown up, and when had she reached the age to sow her wild oats? Matilda felt that time had passed by in a surreal blur and never seemed to slow down.

She pocketed the money and stepped out into the busy morning. Englischers passed by her without much of a glance as she walked down the concrete sidewalk. The town had taken advantage of the warm weather and planted flowers in the several flower beds that lined the street. The smell of fresh potting soil mingled in the warm March morning.

As she walked along, her thoughts wandered to her earlier conversation with her daughter. What was obvious to the community? She was careful to keep the proper amount of distance between them always, and she diligently reminded Ryan whenever he strode across the line. She knew things could never go back to the way they were during her Rumspringa days even if he did not. She had felt the same surge of attraction bubbling throughout the past few months whenever Ryan caught her eye or whenever he sent her one of those secret smiles he had for her alone that he never shared with the rest of the community. Those little smiles, she thought, they were —

They couldn't be with one another, and she slammed shut the tendril of tender hope trying to push forward. This could not be *Gott's* plans for her. Samuel had been the one *Gott* designed for her to love and to be with forever. Except he was gone, and she was left wondering if her sins had come back to haunt her in every way possible, in Samuel's death and in the form of Ryan's presence. She felt her heart crack open as a flood of pain rose.

"Matilda?"

She stopped in mid-step at the sound of Eli's voice, and turned to find him emerging from the hardware store carrying a small paper bag. She had avoided Eli as much as possible since the beginning of January. When they did interact, she kept it as formal and friendly as possible. She felt a bit of guilt gnaw on her conscious as their last conversation occurred prior to Ryan's decision to join the community. Eli approached her and she winced at the sight of the slight frown marring his sun-burned face. More gray had appeared in his hair and beard since the harsh winter. She fought the leap of compassion and concern and simply asked him how he was. She didn't wish to give him hope when there was none.

"What are you doing out of the bakery in the middle of the morning?" he asked.

"My *maemm* sent me to buy some vanilla for the bakery. Our supplies have been growing lower with sales and not keeping track of what we need."

It never failed, she thought. The start of the spring season meant tourism for the town of Monte Vista, and Rebecca's bakery was a frequent stop for many Englischers. Her reputation for delicious baked goods had rapidly spread over the past few years. While they managed to keep up with orders, the constant flow of customers made it hard to keep up with their supplies. Yesterday, they had run out of brown sugar and Lily had been the one to quickly run to the local grocery store.

"I imagine. It's been a busy start of the spring." Eli commented.

"*Ja.*"

They fell into an awkward silence with a spring breeze caressing them. Matilda fidgeted on the balls of her feet nervously, and kept her gaze focused on the steady stream of people walking past them. She looked up when Eli cleared his throat, and stuck his thumbs through the straps of his suspenders. His button-up blue shirt was stained with what looked like oil, and the knees of his trousers were well worn to the point there was almost holes. The sleeves were rolled up over his forearms, and the dips around his fingernails were filled with dirt. He was still ruggedly handsome, even covered in dirt.

"So, how are you?" he asked, his voice sounding a little less confident.

"I'm fine. Everything's fine. How about you?"

"*Gut.* Mostly, at least."

She opened her mouth to ask how his *kinner* were, but decided it was best not to broach the subject. Talking about their *kinner* had always been a way of them connecting to one another." How is your job? Better now that you don't have to work in the cold winter, I bet."

Eli smiled thinly at that. "Much better, I'll admit. Betty has been *gut* about cooking warm meals for when I return home. I don't know what I will do without her once she goes on her Rumspringa."

She caught a brief glimpse of his warm eyes turning misty before they looked away to hide those emotions. Matilda had the urge to rub the spot on her stomach where

her guilt continued to gnaw away and winced at the ache of
it.

"I am sure that Betty wouldn't leave without knowing
you were taken care of," she answered, wishing that she
could avoid the subject.

"*Nee*, she wouldn't, but I do not wish for her to hold
back in starting her own life because of me. I only want
what's best for her."

Matilda's thoughts went to Rosella at work in the fabric
store, most likely pouring over the various fabrics with
awe. "*Ja*. I think all of us want that."

She smiled affectionately at the image of Rosella's offering a carefree smile, coupled with a fire dancing in her eyes.

Eli broke her reverie. "And Rosella? How is she doing?
I have seen her working in the fabric store."

"She's doing *gut*. It's hard to imagine that our girls will
be going on Rumspringa soon."

"It is hard to imagine."

The brown bag crinkled loudly in Eli's hands as he
shifted. He wiped at his brow with the back of his hand
and a rare smile graced his rugged face. "I better go. I have
to return to work, but it was *gut* seeing you, Matilda."

"*Ja*, it was *gut* seeing you as well."

Eli took a step in the opposite direction, but paused for
a second and turned his head to gaze at her over his shoulder. "I pray that we can be friends again someday. I miss
having you around."

Then he simply walked away, down the sidewalk, before
she could reply. Matilda pinched the bridge of her nose
with a sigh and turned to head back in the direction of the
grocery store. She truly missed their friendship, but she

knew Eli well. He had prayed that their friendship could turn in something more.

Matilda was so lost in thought that she failed to notice her feet had unconsciously taken her down a side road to a run-down building. Tears flooded Matilda's eyes as she took in the buggies lined up in front of the building and spare wooden wheels stacked neatly in the small shop attached to an office. The shop door was wide open to let in the fresh air, and the walls were covered with neatly organized shelves. A tall figure stood hunched over the main carriage and the clink of a hammer hitting a nail echoed in the air.

For more than a year Matilda had successfully avoided Samuel's buggy repair shop. Just looking upon it jerked the knife that was embedded deep within her heart. Though he was gone, a part of her expected him to come walking out with a smile on his face. Instead, it was Jacob Byler, a friend of Samuel's, who stepped out of the shop and looked at her in apparent surprise.

"Matilda?" he called out. "What are you doing here?"

Matilda had not recovered from the image of the tall figure bent over the carriage and the corresponding pain in her heart and the way the pain lodged in her throat when that figure slowly turned toward her. The now-faint image of Samuel was replaced by a newer, more familiar man, one with sweat dripping down his tanned forehead. She couldn't help but notice the smudge of oil on Ryan's right cheek. He didn't do anything but stare, perhaps surprised at her presence, too, at the buggy shop.

Maybe it was the grief that dictated what happened next, or it was the nausea rolling through her like a silent threat, but she turned on her heel and ran in the opposite direction, putting distance between her past and the present.

The rest of the afternoon sweated away into a warm evening with the distant click of sprinklers in the fields. Matilda took solace in pruning her garden plot to ready it for planting next weekend. With each distinct rip of roots ripping free from the earth, the weight on her mind eased. When she was finished, a fine layer of sweat had gathered at her hairline and tickled down the curve of her back.

Above the Sangre de Cristo mountain range, more dark clouds congregated around the mountain peaks. Booms of thunder could be felt in the air as a springtime storm made its way down to the valley.

"Are we in for a spring storm?"

Rosella stood on the front porch shielding a hand over her eyes. In her other hand, she clutched a glass of water that sweated in her grasp. Matilda's heart lifted to hear the sound of Rosella's voice addressing her for the first time since their earlier conversation.

Matilda straightened from where she was crouched over her garden, dusting her hands free from weeds and dirt. "Appears so. We should get the horses into the barn if it downpours."

"I guess. Seems unusual with how early this heat and storm arrived." Rosella set her glass down on the porch railing. Gravel crunched underneath her sneakers as she walked towards Matilda.

"*Maemm...*" Rosella started, twirling the edge of her apron with a finger, "I wanted to tell you that I'm sorry for the past couple of weeks."

Matilda gathered Rosella into a forgiving hug. She pressed a cheek into the soft fabric of Rosella's prayer *kapp* and inhaled the soap that still clung to her skin. "All is forgiven. I'm just glad you are talking to me again."

They pulled back with Matilda's hands rubbing her daughter's shoulders soothingly. Rosella offered her a timid smile. "I was upset because of what everyone is saying about you and Ryan. I didn't know what to think."

The wind picked up speed, and this time it felt chillier. It tore at the skirts of their dresses, and their skin prickled in response to the temperature change. Matilda started towards the field where Isaac and Matthew were playing, oblivious to the storm gathering on the horizon. Rosella caught up with her with a few strides of her long legs.

Without breaking her stride, Matilda offered comfort to her daughter. "Just know that I'll always love your *daed,* and there is no replacing him. No matter what others say"

Rosella persisted. "So you don't have any feelings for Ryan then?"

Matilda glanced over at her daughter walking gracefully alongside her in her gray dress and white apron. Her face was impassive as she focused those sapphire eyes of hers on her two *bruders* who were dodging the sprinklers in the field. Her daughter was not going to let it go. "Why are you so curious about this? I've told you that we are only friends."

The rusted gate leading to the field pushed open underneath Matilda's hand with a loud squeak. Dry grass tickled the inside of her knuckles as she walked along the fence toward her sons.

Rosella shrugged noncommittally. "He just seems to really like you particularly, and he is intent on becoming a part of this community. How many Englischers do that? Plus, it seems like all the girls here are in love with him," she said. "It's actually pretty annoying."

"Not many," Matilda agreed, while trying to keep a small smile from showing at her daughter's proclaimed annoyance and trying to juggle against a sudden jealous twinge, "but, Rosella, as I said, he doesn't like me like that. I'm viewed as a friend or a spiritual advisor and that's all."

"*Ja*, but I'm pretty sure Ryan doesn't like you as a friend. It's obvious when a boy is into you."

"*Ach* really?" She turned to look at Rosella who flushed brightly underneath her gaze. "Would you care to elaborate how you know this?"

"I-I-I don't know from personal experience. All the boys here look at me as one of them."

Matilda bit the inside of her cheek to choke down a laugh at the displeasure shown on her daughter's face. She remembered all too well being the same age and wishing that she could start courting so the other boys wouldn't see her as one of them. Samuel had been the only one who seemed to recognize that.

Finally she offered her daughter some hope. "Someday, you will make someone a very happy *mann*, Rosella. It'll be the last person you expect."

"Like you and *daed*?" Rosella asked, visibly brightening. "Didn't you say that *daed* was determined to court you before and after Rumspringa?"

Far more than simply wishing to be with her, Matilda thought, and couldn't help herself when she reached out again to tuck an errant strand of hair behind her daughter's ear. She smiled lovingly at her daughter who had been a blessing from *Gott,* no matter the consequences of her own sinful behavior.

"*Ja.* He was very determined to court me, but I wasn't sure if I could court him. I finally gave in after Rumspringa when I realized he was, indeed, the one *Gott* intended for me."

Rosella's face showed every emotion. "And you were married after that?"

"We were married after that."

Matilda saw Rosella's eyes fill with unshed tears at the story. Together they gathered the horses, along with a protesting Matthew and Isaac. The steady trickle of fat rain drops echoed on the barn roof when they had the horses in the stall until the storm passed, and they all safely entered the *haus.* While her *kinner* gathered in the living room, Matilda opened the windows to allow in the welcoming smell of rain. She so loved the rain and believed it was one of *Gott's* special graces. She inhaled deeply.

The gray clouds above were anything but dreary. A static charge filled the air, and it filled Matilda with an indescribable energy. A ray of sunlight peeked through the twisting clouds. She tilted her head upwards to the sky, and smiled at the feeling of *Gott* there in middle of the storm. No matter how unpredictable the weather could be, or how stormy it could get, *Gott* was above all of it watching on.

Her peace, however, didn't last long. As she had previously predicted, the early bout of hot air didn't last throughout the night. Colorado weather remained unpredictable all year around, and the drastic changes of hot to cold often resulted in some sort of head cold.

Matilda woke as pale morning light spilled in from the window, and violent shivers wracked her limbs from the frigid air. She wrapped a thick blanket around herself, and shoved her bare feet into a pair of Samuel's old boots before hurrying down the hall to check on her *kinner*. The outline of their bodies showed they were curled up tightly under their blankets, but a gentle brush of her hand told her their bodies were warm. Even though her *kinner* protested, she insisted that they sleep with a heavy blanket until it was late spring and any threat of frost had gone.

The stairs groaned beneath her feet as she plodded down the steps to the living room. She glanced out the window and sucked in a breath at the sight of a light snow dusting the land. Thankfully they had yet to plant. The frost would have surely killed any tender vegetation. With a quick prayer of thanks, Matilda tackled the many morning tasks.

After dropping off her *kinner* at the schoolhouse and Rosella at the fabric store, Matilda gladly stepped into the warm kitchen of the bakery. Lily was busy flouring the counter to roll out pie crusts. "Can you believe this weather?"

Her sister gave a miserable shake of her head. Then Matilda saw how the very tip of Lily's nose was red and heard the congestion in her voice.

"*Nee.* I like the warm weather better. It's just plain cruel to be teased like that."

A wave of concern washed over Matilda. "I'll make you some tea for your throat."

She shrugged out of her coat and hung it on the peg beside the door. "Where is *maemm*?"

Lily nodded toward a nearly empty bag on the floor. "We're almost out of flour," she said and sighed. "One of these days we need to shut the bakery down early to take note of what we need or develop some sort of system so we don't have to keep running to the grocery store."

Matilda's hand barely touched the glass jar that held dried mint leaves when a knock on the back door of the bakery punctuated their conversation. The hinges groaned when it opened, and a blast of cold air blew over them.

She watched as Ryan and Jacob Byler stepped into the warm kitchen. Their tall figures lingered at the back near the kitchen sink. She felt a thread of dread tighten her stomach and slowly dropped her hand from the tea jar. When had those two become *gut* friends?

"Smells wonderful here. We were wondering if we could possibly buy something to eat," Jacob said, respectfully removing his hat. "We'd stop by around lunch time, but we've been pretty busy at the buggy shop with all the repairs going on."

"Sure." Lily wiped her hands free of flour, and smiled at the both them. "What would you like us to make?"

"Sandwiches perhaps? I've always loved the food but I also know how much Ryan loves it because he's always stopping by, so we know we'll get something *gut*," Jacob offered.

Ryan looked away and avoided Matilda's gaze. She then realized Jacob was watching their interaction as he tugged on the edge of his brown beard and gave her a small knowing smile. Her heart lurched. Why was Jacob smiling like that?

"How about I make you both a turkey sandwich for lunch?" she said, hoping to speed things along.

Without sparing anyone another look, Matilda scuttled out the front of the kitchen to grab the turkey breast from the cooler they had added a few years ago to keep their ingredients fresh and cool. The blast of cold air felt good on her warm cheeks as she pulled out the meat and placed it on a cutting board.

"Mattie…."

Once again he'd triggered her exasperation. *Gott*, give me strength, she prayed, and help me not grow angry. "I told you, Ryan, that is not how I'm called here," she answered, keeping her voice low as she sliced more turkey. The strong combined scent of salt, smoke, and pepper tickled her nose as she hurriedly made the sandwiches. She just wanted the two of them out of the kitchen but she couldn't help herself. "What are you doing talking to Jacob about me? You know that he is — was — Samuel's friend, his *best* friend."

The floorboards groaned as she heard the sound of Ryan's boots as he moved closer — not what she wanted or needed. The dirt littering the floor from his muddy boots only increased her annoyance as she knew that she would have to sweep it all up before her *maaem* returned and found all the dirt tracked into the kitchen.

"Yes, all right, I knew Jacob and Samuel were friends before I started working there. I didn't think it would be that big a deal."

"Really? You're here a lot and, apparently, talking about your visits. Why? Don't you realize how that sounds to the community? It implies that we were more than friends, and my own daughter is starting to think the same thing. We —"

A strong hand clamped down on her wrist, and stopped her from putting pickles on their sandwiches. Matilda couldn't help but notice how his fingers had changed over the past few months. They were covered in tough calluses and carried the strength from hard work keeping up a farm and *haus*. The contact between them ignited a sizzling sensation that crept up her arm and only increased her anxiety.

"Relax. I haven't told anyone about us. Let others think what they want."

Matilda tried to move away but the fingers circling her wrist refused to release her. He was forcing her to look at him, to raise her eyes from the sandwiches on the cutting board now covered with shredded lettuce. She felt the start of tears and realized only a few inches of space existed between them. They stood so close that her chest nearly touched his with every breath she took. When she tilted her head upward, he met her gaze. She struggled to regroup her senses, then pulled back, as she reached out to grip the counter to steady herself.

"You don't understand. I grew up in this community, and family is the center of our world. If anyone were to ever find out what happened between us on Rumspringa, they'd be so disappointed. I left Lancaster and Samuel and

I have had a good life here. I'm asking you to respect that it's different here. You can't just say things or stop by my *haus* whenever you want."

"I don't get it. Aside from just visiting a friend, what's wrong with saying something that lets a person know that you are interested in them?"

Matilda decided to ignore his comment and wished she could do as well where he still had her pinned by the wrist. "*Ja*, that is part of it. This is not a pick-and-choose type of life. You can't rebel against certain rules and accept others. If you truly wish to be a part of this community, to be close to *Gott*, you have to accept *all* of it. Not just the parts that fit."

She managed to finally free her wrist from his strong grip and took a step back to put distance between them. Ryan's face displayed a bit of faint annoyance at her distance before an impassive mask slipped on instead.

"Is that what is *really* bothering you?" Ryan asked.

"*Ja*," she said, still trying to keep her anger under control. "It is bothering me. If my *kinner* can see what's going on then I can only imagine what the community sees and thinks."

"*Ach?*"

The sound of the familiar Pennsylvania Dutch language common to her community slipping from Ryan's tongue caused her to experience a few shivers, but she shrugged in an attempt to keep Ryan from noting her true reaction. She didn't want him to know the panic that surged through her whenever he took a daring step forward to decrease the distance between them.

"What is going on, Mattie," he asked, exasperation clearly showing in his voice and stance. "I'd really like to know what you think is going on. Are you upset because I mentioned how much I like the food here or are you worried about my friendship with Jacob or is there something else?"

"I-I-I —", she was at lost for words. She didn't know where to begin or how or even what to say. She wasn't even sure she knew her own mind.

Still in a quandary, Matilda watched as a small smile play around Ryan's mouth. She couldn't stop looking. His hand reached toward her. For a moment, she wondered what kind of game he was playing but the rest of her urged caution and pushed her to flee before things could get out of hand. Their finger tips gently touched, then held a moment before her tense fingers parted to let his lace through. Butterflies found a new home within her stomach and fluttered so hard it left her breathless with how torn she felt between excitement and fear.

For the briefest of moments, Matilda recognized how tired she was: tired of erecting fences, tired of maintaining boundaries, tired of keeping her distance. She knew in her heart of hearts that Ryan exerted the same pull on her as he had so many years ago. They were palm to palm now, and she felt him move in toward her.

The moment crashed down upon them as if it were scattered shards of glass when the door opened behind them. Ryan took a quick step backward, but his fingers remained threaded through hers when they both turned to see Rosella.

"*Maemm?* Isaac is sick, and…" Rosella trailed off at the sight of their joined hands.

Matilda snatched her hand away quickly from Ryan's as he took another large step back and cleared his throat. "Matilda started to speak. " Rosella ——"

"What is going on?" Rosella demanded, staring openly at Ryan with distrust, then turning toward her mother. "What is going on, *maemm?* Tell me the truth."

Matilda felt the hard stare of her daughter and was unable to meet her daughter's gaze. She swallowed, hard, but still the lump remained. She looked between them, their similar blonde locks and sapphire eyes. It would be so easy to tell them both together, some part of her reasoned.

CHAPTER FOUR

Rosella and Ryan hadn't moved or said a word when Matilda opened her mouth to speak. "I was just making Ryan and Jacob some sandwiches for their lunch breaks," she said, hearing the hollowness of her words.

The half-finished sandwiches sat on the counter. Apparently, she'd scattered the pickles on more than the sandwiches when she and Ryan began their talk. They dotted the cutting board and counter, too. At first Rosella didn't express any emotion, but that changed when she focused on Ryan. Her suspicion and distrust was obvious from the look on her face to the way she held herself. It pained Matilda to see her daughter's response toward Ryan. It was a hard tug on her heart.

Rosella continued to stare at Ryan. "What do you want with my *maemm?*" she demanded.

Matilda felt Ryan stiffen at Rosella's confrontational reaction. Since Samuel's death, Rosella had grown even more protective over her family, but Matilda had always been quick to reprimand her for such behavior. Being confrontational was never welcome by anyone in the community for any reason.

"Rosella. You know not to confront people and especially community members."

At first, Rosella didn't respond to Matilda's scolding but then Matilda saw that raised eyebrow given to him in a silent challenge. Matilda had enough. Bad enough that her flushed body still betrayed her as a result of what had transpired earlier with Ryan, but she wouldn't and couldn't allow this situation to stand between Ryan and Rosella. Without another word or look, Matilda brushed past him and focused on her daughter.

"What's the matter with Matthew?"

Thankfully, Matilda's question distracted Rosella who turned her attention to the back door of the bakery and nodded. "He's complaining of a sore throat and a runny nose. Lucy's *maemm* brought him to the fabric store after dropping off her *kinner* at school."

Her words stirred Matilda into action. "We'll have to wait for a minute until your *Grohs-mammi* gets back. Where is he now?"

"Outside in the buggy."

Matilda fought the irritation at Rosella leaving her *bruder* alone, and apparently sick, in the buggy outside. Although she still felt full of confusing emotions whipped up by Ryan and Rosella, Matilda focused on the new problem at hand. With hasty movements, she finished making the turkey sandwiches and wrapped them securely in parchment paper.

"Here," she said and placed them a bit roughly into Ryan's outstretched hands, careful to avoid any more contact. "Don't worry about the money. I have to go."

She didn't give him a chance to answer. Rebecca entered the front of the bakery, and Matilda gave her a quick rundown of Matthew's condition. Avoiding any chance of questions from Rebecca, she nodded at Ryan and told her mother of his need to pay for the sandwiches and left them together.

Matilda ushered Rosella through the kitchen, while ignoring Lily's concerned inquiries and Jacob's questioning look. She knew her actions were in part for her concern over her son's well being but also driven by her strong need for distance between herself and Ryan. Her apprehension immediately evaporated at the sight of Matthew's pale face stretched into misery as he sat huddled on the front seat of their family buggy.

"You should not have left him out here in the cold, Rosella."

The words came out as an unintended snap. Matilda hurriedly wrapped a quilted blanket they kept stashed in the buggy for the cold season around Matthew's shoulders, and swept a concerned hand across his pale forehead. The heat of his skin was a stark contrast to the chill in the air and a major concern.

"He has a fever," Matilda said, and turned to look at Rosella. "I need you to stay here to help your *Grohs-mami* with the bakery while I care for Matthew. Make sure to pick up your *bruder* from the schoolhouse and bring him back to the bakery."

Matilda didn't give Rosella any opportunity to argue. She gathered the reins in her hands, without thinking to go back and get her coat. With a firm flick of the reins and a cluck of her tongue, she had them pulling away from the bakery with steady hoofbeats. Dark clouds had already gathered on the horizon, and the air felt even chillier. She felt the hair on her arms rise as thunder boomed from mountain tops as the rapidly approaching storm swept in on a strong gust of wind.

When they reached the edge of Monte Vista, a heavy sheet of rain crashed down upon them with a loud thunderous boom. Her pale gray dress was a dark blur, almost the color of her mourning clothes, and she felts the strands of her hair plastered to the sides of her cold cheeks. The smell of dry dirt gave away quickly to a rich, damp smell of wet hay as they passed fields.

Matthew sat shivering alongside her, the dark strands of his hair plastered to his pale forehead. Lightning flashed above them followed by a loud crack that startled Pepper from his steady trot down the gravel road leading to their *haus*. Matilda was quick to regain control and steered them into the comfort of the barn.

"Mama, I'm cold," Matthew said, his teeth clattering to prove his point. "I thought it was supposed to be warm."

Peeling away the thoroughly soaked blanket from his trembling shoulders, Matilda draped it across the side of the carriage to dry and be washed later. "It's not yet summer, Matthew. It's still early spring, and the threat of the cold hasn't gone away yet."

Despite her chilled fingers, she somehow unbuckled Pepper from the buggy and led him to a stall with a bucket of grain and a pail of water. She helped Matthew stiffly climb down from the buggy, and together they sprinted back into the dark morning towards the *haus*. When they reached the back porch, she lingered back knowing that they would need wood to start a fire in the wood stove.

She urged Mathew into the *haus*. "Go inside, and change your clothes. I'll be right there."

Mud squished beneath her sneakers as she made her way around the side of the *haus* where there was still a supply of chopped firewood. Matilda paused in front of the small pile as her thoughts went back to her earlier interaction with Eli. A pang of guilt flared when she remembered the previous fall when Eli spent two Saturdays chopping wood so they would be able to keep warm during the winter season. Then, without rhyme or reason, her thoughts traveled to what had transpired earlier in the bakery with Ryan's fingers threading through her own. She felt a sudden surge of heat spread, making her skin feel hot and feverish against the cold rain.

Refusing to allow anymore distractions, Matilda grabbed an armful of chopped wood and hurried back inside to warm the chilled *haus*. By the time her mother arrived with Rosella and Isaac, Matilda had Matthew tightly bundled in a thick blanket as he dozed off on the couch in front of the wood stove.

"How is he doing?" Rebecca asked as she opened the front door.

"He has a fever," Matilda answered, rushing over to open the door further so they could get out of the cold. "I'm praying that his fever will break while he sleeps. *Danka* for dropping Rosella and Isaac off. Was the bakery busy?"

The steady patter of rain on the porch roof was a soothing sound, but the chill that clung to them from outside erased any sort of comfort. A deep seed of dread had planted itself in Matilda at the rapid change of weather. It was a sure sign that they were going to battle a cold spring despite the earlier bout of heat.

"Nothing we couldn't handle," Rebecca said and turned to Rosella and Isaac who were stamping off the cold rain. "Be mindful to your *maemm* and be quiet for your *bruder*. He's sleeping off his fever."

"Go change out of your damp clothes," Matilda added, taking Isaac's wet hat from his head. In her concerned and confused state, she didn't even feel annoyed by her *maemm* ordering her *kinner* around.

A dripping Rosella lingered in the hallway as Isaac stomped up the stairs to change out of his own wet clothes. She peered around the doorframe leading into the living room before turning to look at Matilda with concern. "Will Matthew be okay?"

"I'm sure he will be once we rid him of the fever. Now, go on. Get upstairs and change. I don't want all you *kinner* to get sick."

Still, Rosella stayed. "I'm sorry that I left him in the buggy — and for my behavior earlier. I-I didn't think about it."

Before Matilda could answer, shame colored Rosella's face and she darted up the stairs to the confines of her own bedroom. Matilda stood ramrod stiff as she waited for Rebecca, who had remained by the slightly open door, to either question her or leave.

"What happened at the bakery before Rosella arrived?"

Matilda nearly rolled her eyes at how predictable her *maemm* could be at times. Not in the mood to discuss it, she schooled her features into a nonchalant expression. "Nothing happened. I was making sandwiches for Jacob and Ryan."

"Matilda," Rebecca started with a sigh, shaking her head. "All I ask is that you protect yourself and your *kinner* from another heartbreak."

A cold breeze traveled inside and bit at Matilda's ankles as it trailed down the hallway. She avoided her *maemm's* gaze by nodding her head. "You probably should go home, *maemm*, before the weather gets worse."

For a moment, Matilda thought her mother might come inside to continue their conversation, but instead she opened the door and stepped out into the rainy afternoon. Matilda lingered at the door to watch her mother climb safely into her buggy and turn around on the road to return home. When she finally softly closed the door behind her, Matilda rested her forehead against the grainy wood.

"*Gott,* help me weather this."

Four long days passed with stormy weather that brought cold rain and nippy breezes. Matilda stood in front of the kitchen sink waiting for the water to come to a boil on the stove as she took in the dreary morning. Dark clouds continued to dump rain in large quantities, and while the grass seemed to green up overnight, the cold temperatures at night had shocked the fruit trees. The fields were a muddy mess compared to how dry they had been a couple days ago, and Matilda saw the evidence of that trailing down her hallway from Rosella's boots when her daughter returned from feeding their animals.

The sizzle of water splashing onto the stovetop drew her attention back to the stove. With careful fingers, she poured the boiling water into a small cup before placing the peppermint tea leaves in to steep. Along with the four days of non-stop cold rain, Matthew's fever had persisted with it rarely breaking. His body constantly went from cold to hot and a fine layer of sweat covering his skin at all times.

Her heart ached for her youngest child. The events in the bakery still plagued her, but she managed to shove them away during the times Matthew was awake. She had yet to see Ryan since that day and was inwardly relieved to have the distance.

When the smell of peppermint filled her lungs, Matilda held the bowl of ice cubes she had grabbed from the ice box in the pantry below the *haus*. She plopped a few pieces of ice into the hot liquid and listened to the light crackling of the cubes as they submerged into the hot tea.

The stairs groaned underneath her boots as she made her way to where Matthew lay in bed, staring miserably out the window while curled up in a blanket. Matilda sat on the edge of the bed and absently tugged the blankets more firmly around him.

"Here. This is peppermint, and it'll help with your throat."

Matthew glanced at the cup of tea before scowling. "I don't like peppermint."

She ignored the surly attitude, knowing her youngest son was merely acting out of misery. Gently nudging his arm, Matilda smiled down at him as she used her free hand to push back some strands of hair from his forehead. He would need a haircut soon, she thought.

"You only have to take a couple of drinks. It'll help, I promise."

Settling up against the headboard and pillows, he took the cup of peppermint tea with an impatient sigh. He shifted in his cotton shirt, now damp from the fever sweats. She watched as he took a couple of gulps of tea before handing it back with a grimace.

Matilda couldn't help but worry given all that happened with Samuel but she tried to maintain a confident air when speaking to Mathew. "How are you feeling? Better?"

"*Nee*. I hurt everywhere," he complained, slipping back down between the blankets and sheets.

"You haven't eaten in a while. I'll make us some soup for dinner with fresh bread. How does that sound?"

Matthew shrugged his answer. She waited until he fell asleep, rubbing small circles on his back, before venturing back down to the kitchen. While she chopped an onion and then threw the pieces into a large pot to brown, her thoughts began to wander, returning once more to *Gott's* plan for her life.

Surely, *Gott* did not intend for them to be together. Not after losing Samuel, nor with Ryan still adjusting to their faith. Their attraction would not end well; she could feel it deep within her heart. Not only was she unsure of Ryan's seriousness in his commitment to *Gott* and their lifestyle, but the community held even deeper doubts. Just the other day she heard Almina, an elderly church member who was notoriously cranky, tell her *maemm*, that *mensleit* like Ryan would never be able to live a pure life.

Up until then that thought had never crossed Matilda's mind. They were attracted to one another, she couldn't deny that, but she also knew that whatever indiscretions Ryan held within the past would hinder him. The lines in social behavior within their community were blurry to him, such as his holding her hand in the bakery. Her ears burned thinking of how *wunderbar* it had felt to have some- one else's fingers threaded through her own. She tried to picture Ryan then fitting into their lives, sitting in Samuel's chair at the head of the table, removing Samuel's old clothes to make room for his.

Matilda sucked in a watery breath and returned to the present where she stirred the onions around until they were evenly golden brown before adding some beans and four cups of milk. Sprinkling bits of salt and pepper to the bubbling liquid, she cubed a couple of bread slices to add to the soup, something her *kinner* always loved.

Rosella arrived with Isaac as the rain pattered even harder on the roof. They waved a quick hand to Rebecca, protected by an umbrella and sitting in the buggy, before gladly slinking into the warm *haus*. Matilda nodded a word- less *danka* in her *maemm's* direction before closing the door behind them. Given the weather, she knew her *maemm* would hurry home.

Isaac raised his head and sniffed. "Is that church soup I smell?"

"*Ja*. Go upstairs and change before dinner. Then help your *bruder* come down the stairs. He needs to eat."

Isaac shrugged out of his coat before handing it to Ma- tilda to hang up a wooden peg and darted up the stairs with all the grace and energy that Matilda wished she had at the end of the day.

"How is Matthew?" Rosella asked, shrugging out of her own coat and hanging it on a peg. "Did his fever finally break?"

Matilda lightly shook Isaac's coat free of the rain drops still clinging to it. "*Nee.* It has been off and on all day still. If the fever has not let up by tonight, I will have to go to Mark Bender to see whether he can look at Matthew."

Rosella looked over at her in alarm. "The doctor? Is it that bad, *maemm?* I'm really sorry for leaving him in the cold. I —"

"Shh, Rosella. I am sure Matthew will be fine, but I have done all that I can do to help the fever. Mark is our doctor, and he will know more to help Matthew if things don't get better. Now, help me set the table so we can eat."

As they ate together, the storm continued to rage on with flashes of lightning followed by loud cracks of thunder. Matilda continued to watch Matthew as he took a few bites and couldn't help but be disappointed when he then promptly pushed the bowl away. She noticed the fine layer of sweat covering his face again, too, and felt her heart twist helplessly at the sight. She didn't like to leave her *kinner* during this unusual spring storm to travel to Mark Bender's but would if she must. As the community's local doctor his *haus* had to be miles down the road and a trip she did not want to make.

"I don't think you need to worry about watering the fields for a while," Rosella said, her voice breaking through Matilda's thoughts. Rosella placed her hands on the edge of the sink and peered out through the window. "I have never seen such a bad storm before. Have you *maemm?*"

Matilda hurriedly gathered the dishes from the table as Isaac helped Matthew up the stairs and back to their shared bedroom. She set them on the counter next to Rosella and glanced out the window as well with trepidation. The land around them was smothered in a wet darkness; not even the mountains were visible in the distance. The light from the lantern inside the barn was a blurry blob in the surrounding darkness.

"I hate to take Pepper out in this but I must," she said. "Stay here with your *bruders* and do your best to keep Matthew's fever down."

"Are you sure?" Rosella questioned, following on Matilda's heels into the hallway. "This storm is getting worse by the minute, and you know Pepper hates lightening."

Matilda caught sight of the fear spreading across her daughter's face, and paused in slipping on her coat. With a gentle hand, she cupped that smooth cheek she knew so well and smiled. So many freckles from being out in the sun over the past few weeks danced their way across the sharp pop of Rosella's cheekbones.

"I'll be fine, Rosella. Just watch your *bruders,* and I'll be back shortly. I promise."

The downpour of the rain outside drowned out Rosella's reply. Matilda shut the door behind her, and tugged the hood of her jacket over her prayer *kapp*. Somehow she managed to convince a spooked Pepper out of the barn to be hitched, and then lured him to go out into the storming evening.

Rain drops stung her cheeks and beat down on her shoulders. Matilda clutched at the hood of her coat, desperately peering out at the dismal surroundings as Pepper trotted uneasily along to Mark Bender's *haus*. A flash of lightening from above startled Pepper, and he immediately reared up at the bright light.

"Easy, Pepper! Keep going," she said, working to guide the horse forward.

Her determination strengthened despite the uneasiness from the violence of the storm. This time, she thought to herself with clenched teeth, there would be no delay in getting help. Not when Matthew's fever continued to worsen. The similarities between Samuel and Matthew left her sick with agony. She would not sit by this time and pray that *Gott* would heal him like she had done with Samuel.

The hair on the back of her neck stood on edge as they rounded a muddy turn. Reins gripped in her fingers, Matilda spotted the blurry shape of another buggy parting through the rain. She opened her mouth to call out, but the blinding light dancing across the sky stopped her in midcall.

Pepper reared up again in fright and resisted all of Matilda's commands and attempts to soothe. Time slowed as the buggy wheels slid down into a steep ditch with Pepper thrashing wildly against the harness. Cold fear shot up Matilda's spine as she felt her seat tip to the right, then the muffled sound of wood groaned against her ear as gravity urged the teetering buggy to fall onto its side. She opened her mouth and screamed as the reins slipped from her fingers, and she tumbled out onto the rocky ground.

Her last memory before her head collided with a jutting rock was of the barbed wire fence cutting into her side and the sound of her dress ripping before a darkness quickly swallowed her.

CHAPTER FIVE

L ost in darkness, Matilda dreamt of a warm summer morning in a forest glade high on the mountain side. The smell of dry pine needles tickled her nose as she stepped cautiously through a tangle of green foliage. Small branches snagged in the folds of her light blue dress, and when she made to free herself a familiar calloused hand was already there.

She accepted the offered hand and a soft voice urged her forward. "Be as careful as you can, Matilda. I don't want you to get scratched."

She paused for a moment as she felt her heart cramp in agony as the voice washed over her and the hand dropped away. A hot breeze blew past her and accompanied quiet, quick footsteps. When she turned, she found a tall figure leaning against a wide tree.

"Samuel?" she whispered.

No sign of paleness in his smooth and tanned pallor remained. He was well groomed with his raven locks cut short and not a strand of his beard out of place. His white button-down shirt was wrinkle free, and his thumbs hooked casually in the bands of his suspenders. Samuel gave her a loving smile as the sunlight revealed the contours of the handsome face she missed and loved so dearly.

A part of her recognized that this had to be a dream, but it was a good dream compared to all those other nightmares of his death that plagued her nights. She wanted it to never end.

Samuel rested a hand on a tree branch above his head and looked around the glade before he spoke. "You look *gut*, Matilda. Do you remember this place?"

"Is this a dream? Or am I dead?" she asked, unsure whether she actually voiced the words. She closed her eyes.

Flashes of lightening, wood groaning before it splintered, and Pepper's terrified whinnying broke through.

With a frightening fury, it all came back. Images played across her closed eyes. She wanted to go to Samuel, to run to safety. She felt her hand rise, as if disconnected from her body, and seeking Samuel but the movement stopped when their *kinner's* faces flashed forward.

She felt great pain and cried out. "Our *kinner*, Samuel... They will be heartbroken if I am dead too."

"Shhh, Matilda. You are not dead; only asleep."

A wave of relief flooded through her. She wanted to reach out, and graze her finger tips along the buttons of his shirt. She sought the warmth of his skin, the steady rise of his chest, and the thump of his heart. Her fingertips tingled and yet they remained centimeters away from her desire.

"Tell me you remember this place, Matilda," Samuel repeated.

Matilda forced her eyes away from him to take in forest. Her heart softened as she recalled the time that Samuel had taken her up to this glade to confess that he loved her. Sunlight trickled down upon them through the whispering pine trees, and birds chirped peacefully from the upper branches above them. The tall columbines and swaying grass tickled the skin of her calves.

"I remember. This is where you told me that you loved me."

Samuel smiled and gazed fondly around the wild clearing. "I still love you, Matilda. I think about you and our *kinner* always. I have been watching over all of you since I joined our Heavenly Father."

Matilda's heart ripped apart, torn between shame for her behavior with Ryan and relief at knowing Samuel still loved and protected them. What if she's been wrong? What if she has no place in *Gott's* plan for Ryan? What if *Gott* does not want her to help him? Could she be so wrong?

"You look worried," Samuel said. He smiled when Matilda glanced upwards at him, still gnawing on her bottom lip. "What troubles you?"

Matilda couldn't bear the love flowing from Samuel any longer and lowered her eyes in shame. Tears poured forth. Shame filled her. "I have not been a *gut maemm* or person —ever. I do not deserve your love and protection."

"Don't be so hard on yourself, Matilda. We did what we had to do at the time to assure your future within the community and to live according to *Gott's* will. Look at *Gott's* blessing that we received in return."

"Maybe, but that doesn't mean my feelings are right today. I don't know what they are anymore. I love you, and I miss you with everything —"

"You have a second chance for what you wanted in the first place," Samuel finished for her.

Matilda shook her head in confusion, a tidal wave of emotions threatening to break through her. "I don't think it was even what I wanted in the first place. It doesn't matter now. I want you. I want you to come back. It's not fair that you had to leave, and I had to stay behind."

Her voice wavered with pent up emotions. In three graceful steps, Samuel had his arms wound gently around her quivering frame and her head found its place against his chest. He still smelled of the fresh wood and wood stain that followed him home from work every evening. The steady thrum of his heart beat felt all too real and a little cruel given that this was some sort of dream, the type of dream she had longed for all these months during the long plague of nightmares. It hit her then hard how much she had missed feeling his arms around her, and his chin sitting rightly on top of her head.

"Blessed are those who mourn," Samuel whispered, rubbing soothing circles across her back with his palms. "I always knew that there had been something more with him. Nothing that I could ever compete with but only prayed that you could maybe one day feel that way about me."

"I do feel that way for you!" Matilda insisted and wrapped him more tightly within her arms, unwilling to let go of him. "How could you think such a thing? I love you, and only you."

"Matilda," Samuel started with a sigh, freeing her hands from where they were currently clutching the back of his shirt. As their eyes met, he took both of her hands in his, rubbing calloused thumbs across the back of her knuckles. "I would never want you to deny yourself another chance of happiness or love because you were afraid of judgment, or what I would feel. I am proud of you for being as strong as you have been. If he can provide for you, be a *gut daed* to our *kinner*, then I am happy."

Her very soul ached at his goodness. "He's not you though, Samuel. You are my *mann*."

"And I am not he, either, Matilda. You have to let go of one of us to have the other."

Matilda swallowed thickly and couldn't answer. She sought his face and tried to read his carefully guarded expression. Finally, she got the words out: "What are you saying?"

"Do the right thing, Matilda. Do what your heart is telling you to do. *Gott* is with you as I am too."

With that, his hands slipped from hers, and he stepped backwards, away from her. A sad smile graced his face as the foliage around them began to blur and as Matilda felt the dream fade. A deep well of pain opened up inside her, and she reached out toward him.

"Don't leave! Samuel, please. Come back to me."

His smile deepened into an even sadder smile. "You know I can't come back. Wake up, Matilda. It's time to wake up now."

A cool rag was draped over her forehead. Trails of water, or tears, dripped down the side of her temples into the pillow cradling her head. Matilda sucked in a harsh breath as she realized that the dream was now gone, and that the agonizing pain within her soul matched her body's physical pain. The cushions beneath her dipped down as someone sat next to her and she felt a strong hand gripping her own.

"Matilda? Can you hear me?"

"*Maemm?*" She croaked out and reached up to touch a tender spot on the back of her head. "Where am I? What happened?"

Matilda's mother called out, "Mark, she's awake." She then stared down at Matilda. "You're in Mark Bender's *haus*, and I am so relieved you are awake."

Grabbing the damp rag, Matilda slid it free from her head. A wave of warm heat touched her aching head, and someone adjusted the quilted blanket around her shoulders. The smell of rubbing alcohol and cleanliness permeated her senses. After several long seconds of squinting to adjust to the lantern light above her, Matilda saw the tall figure stooped over her. Mark Bender's warm brown eyes stared intently into hers as he waved a finger here and there. Up close she could see the faint lines around the corner of his eyes and the threads of gray in his long brown beard.

Mark Bender continued his examination. "How are you feeling, Matilda? Your head took quite a beating."

No doubt, she thought, as her head pounded and pounded. She tried to grit her teeth and stave off the feeling as she sat up, much against the protestations of her mother and the community doctor. She felt a sharp pain in her side and winced.

"Lay still. You have stitches in your side from being tangled up in the barbed wire fence," Mark said and pushed firmly to force her to recline back against the pillows.

Matilda's skin itched at that as she shifted to adjust more comfortably on the small couch and her body voiced its complaint at all her moving. The wood stove crackled happily in the far right corner of the living room while the steady patter of rain echoed throughout the *haus*. She remembered she'd had a dream not a nightmare of Samuel and strained to remember more but couldn't. Try as she might, she couldn't even recall how she arrived at Mark's *haus*.

Somewhat frustrated, Matilda realized she'd have to ask some questions. "How did I get here?"

Rebecca grabbed Matilda's hand and squeezed, and Matilda was surprised to see tears. They glimmered in her *maemm's* eyes as she spoke, "Ryan brought you here. You were lucky that he was nearby to see your accident. You could have died, Matilda. What were you thinking?"

"It was an accident, *maemm*. Pepper reared up, and —"

"The buggy flipped, and it could've flipped right on top of you. I thank *Gott* that Ryan was there at the right time."

A vision of Mathew, hot and sweaty, blew into Matilda's mind. "What about Matthew? He's sick with fever," she said and struggled once again to get up and the quilt slipped to the floor. "We have to get to him. Rosella is with them. My *kinner* —"

"I have sent my *fraa* to attend your children, along with medicine. Your *maemm* had mentioned that Matthew has been sick for the past four days. Don't worry," Mark said, tucking the quilt back in place.

"He's all right?"

Mark smiled, his body relaxed but his voice firm. "Not to worry," he repeated. "Matthew is fine, Matilda. All is fine. Please, lay still while I steep you some ginger tea to help with your pain. I'll be back with more ice for that huge bird's egg at the back of your head, too."

With a quick squeeze of Rebecca's shoulder, Mark Bender left them alone in the tiny living room. Matilda sank back against the pillows, pressing a hand to her aching head. The non-stop pounding was getting worse. The accident, the dream, it all left her feeling surreally out of place with reality. She felt herself begin to drift, so she decided to talk to keep herself grounded and unable to float back into any kind of dreamless sleep that would rob her of her faculties. She had to stay present — for Mathew.

She looked at Rebecca. "How did you get here? You shouldn't have gone out in this weather, either. Look what happened to me."

"That's not funny, Matilda, and it was Ryan who came to our doorstep after bringing you here to Mark. He brought me here to be with you. T'was *Gott's* will for him to be there, for you."

It took a moment for Matilda to take that all in. After all, how many times had her *maemm* voiced her distrust towards Ryan because of his sometimes worldly behavior and charming tongue? Yet, she could see that a bit of that distrust had melted ever so slightly.

Rebecca sat, back ramrod straight, hand clasping Matilda's hand, and focused solely on her daughter. She tilted her head and asked, "Why are you looking at me so strangely?"

"I'm just surprised is all. You sound as though you've changed your mind about Ryan. I didn't think you would."

Rebecca scoffed out a disapproving sound and pointedly avoided Matilda's gaze as she straightened the blanket across her body. "*Ja*, well," she mumbled, "I might have changed my mind. How could I not be grateful to him for saving your life?"

Matilda turned to look around the room, suddenly realizing Ryan's absence. "Where is he?"

"He left a few minutes ago to retrieve your *daed*. We'll need the extra help to get you back home."

Matilda felt her cheeks flame hot at the thought of Ryan seeing her in the state of tangled mess she was in when the buggy rolled. Subtly, she lifted the quilt to take in her tattered dress with its stains of blood and her bare feet. The strands of her hair felt loose from its usual bun and an examining hand assured her that her prayer *kapp* was indeed gone.

Although she was grateful for Ryan's timely appearance and her apparent rescue, it tugged even harder on her heart strings. While Samuel had encouraged her to let go, to be happy once more, she continued to stubbornly cling to her desire to distance herself. There were too many unanswered questions between them and feelings that could potentially destroy them. Or at least, for herself. While she had always viewed Samuel as a handsome *mann* from his boyish grin, and even considered it about Eli as well for his rugged appearance, Ryan had been a temptation then and now. Simply being near his presence sent her heart racing. "I had a dream about Samuel. Not like any of the other dreams I've had," Matilda blurted out, hoping to distract herself from those last thoughts.

"A dream? What sort of dream?"

"I don't know how to explain it," she said, shifting once again on the cushion. Her side itched horribly from what she assumed to be the stitches. "We were up in the glade, and we were talking as if he was still alive and in front of me. It was like he was reaching out to me."

Rebecca's lips pursed as she contemplated Matilda's outburst. After a few more seconds of what, to Matilda, was an unbearable silence, she spoke. "Maybe this would be better for you to discuss with the Bishop, that is, if you feel so strongly about it. You did hit your head hard on the rocks."

Matilda felt the back of head to gauge whether the goose egg had grown any larger. "You're probably right. It's so strange that I don't even know myself what happened."

Their conversation was interrupted briefly when Mark returned with a steaming cup of ginger tea. Matilda took it with a grateful smile and, with his help, sat up on the couch. The world swayed dizzily for a few long minutes and her head pounded before everything righted itself correctly.

"You're going to need to take it easy for a while, Matilda." Mark started, a warning lacing his voice. "No heavy chores and plenty of rest when you can. You must be careful. I don't want those stitches to get infected, either."

Matilda sipped the tea before she answered, rather weakly, too. "I'll try."

She had just taken her last gulp of ginger tea when a swift set of knocks on the front door echoed throughout the warm *haus*. Her fingers trembled as she set the cup down clumsily on the end table next to the couch and smoothed back wayward strands of hair. When her mother gave her one of those arched eyebrow looks that only she could give, Matilda forced herself to stop while mentally scolding herself for caring about her appearance when Ryan had obviously seen her already.

Jonathan rushed into the living room soon as the door was open. The heavy fabric of his coat was drenched from the downpour of rain, and he swiftly dropped to his knees to hug Matilda fiercely to him. Surprised by the emotion behind it, she tentatively hugged her *daed* back while her eyes met Ryan's. He hung back in the doorframe leading to the hallway, giving them privacy. His own coat was drenched from the downpour, and his face was unusually pale.

She tried to offer him a grateful smile, but he didn't return it. Instead, he dropped his gaze to the floorboards.

"*Danka Gott* that you are all right," Jonathan said, pulling back to smile in relief. "You have given us all quite the scare."

Warmed by the intensity of her father's words, Matilda attempted to paint a softer picture. "I'm honestly fine. All of you, I'll be fine. It was just an accident," she said, offering each a smile. "By next week, we won't even remember this happening."

Her parents exchanged an exasperated look at each other before Jonathan turned to Ryan. "Could you help us, Ryan? We should get her home before the storm gets worse. If she is free to leave, of course," he said to Mark.

"I believe she will be fine. Maybe a headache for a day or two, but try to keep her awake for the next couple of hours to make sure that there is no concussion. If she starts to become unresponsive and sleepy come back immediately," Mark said, nodding his head to each one of them.

Ryan approached the couch. Their eyes met once again, and several emotions too fleeting to read, passed through those cerulean depths of his. He held out a hand for Matilda to take, waiting for her to make the first move. Her heart thundered at the thought of openly being touched by Ryan in front of her parents and a certain hesitancy made itself known. She quickly asserted that his gesture wasn't a public display of affection but an offer of assistance.

She placed her hand in his. He felt warm and strong beneath hers. Ryan eased her up with little effort on his part, and mindful of the stitches that Mark had done on her right side, draped one of her arms across his broad shoulders. A wave of pain from the movement had her clutching the wet fabric of his coat. The skin on her hip tightened and flared when Ryan's hand came to rest there firmly as he guided her on unsteady feet out the door.

Matilda leaned heavily against him as the world swayed, and the pain in her side intensified. Her hand drifted down to where his rested on her hip, and she gripped his thumb as he helped her along the muddy pathway to the buggy. Even with all the damp heavy smell of rain and mud, she could still smell that minty freshness that always clung to him. As cold air rushed to greet her, she clutched at the coat Ryan had slipped over her shoulders to protect her modesty as well as to protect her from the rain.

"Watch your step," Ryan said, his voice heavy and low. "If it hurts, tell me to stop."

She climbed into the buggy, sucking in hard breaths to stave off the pain from all the movement. Ryan then held out a helping hand to Rebecca who took it without any hesitance and settled into the seat alongside Matilda, with

Jonathan sitting behind them. In that moment, with the buggy jerking beneath them, Matilda didn't care if anyone saw that her hand reached out to grab Ryan's for comfort. Her eyes drifted closed when his fingers squeezed hers back, and the dream faded away with the comfort of long nimble fingers threaded through her own.

When they reached the *haus,* all three of her *kinner* were standing outside on the porch with Mark's *fraa* standing behind them. Thankfully, she kept a retrained hand on them to keep them from running out into the yard to greet Matilda.

"Go inside, all three of you," Rebecca shouted. "Inside, Matthew. You are sick with a fever. We'll be in in a minute."

They managed to cross the muddy lawn to the front porch with Ryan's hand still firmly clasped in hers. He only let go once they entered the hallway, when he helped her sit on the couch.

"I'll get some wood for the stove," Jonathan said, slamming the door behind them. "Don't worry about getting up tonight, Matilda. Your *maemm* and I are staying tonight to help you."

"*Danka.* I appreciate it."

Her *kinner* rushed to the couch the second Ryan stepped away. She took in their frightened faces and tear-soaked cheeks with heartfelt prayers to *Gott* for Him to always keep them protected from further fear and heartache.

"I'll be all right," she said, smoothing down a cowlicked strand of hair on Isaac's head. "Go on upstairs, and get to bed. Especially you, Matthew."

Rosella lingered by the couch as her *bruders* pounded up the stairs with Rebecca guiding them along. Without warning, she threw her arms around Matilda's shoulders, and squeezed her tightly. "I'm glad you're okay, *maemm*. I was so worried when Mark's *fraa* arrived to tell us what happened."

Matilda managed to hide her grimace of pain and patted Rosella's slender shoulder. "I'll be fine. I'll need your help —"

"Of course! Anything you need."

They shared a smile before Rosella straightened and turned to face Ryan. For a moment, they regarded each other silently. Matilda's stomach tightened as she watched, trying not to let her nerves gallop away as father and daughter took in each other. Matilda feared the worst.

"*Danka* for saving my *maemm.*"

Ryan gave Rosella a big smile. He nodded his head as Rosella brushed by him with her own tentative smile.

He looked after Rosella for a moment, then shoved his hands deep into his pockets before he spoke. "Looks like I'm starting to be accepted."

Matilda shivered, but she knew it had little to do with the cold rain or with the buggy crash. Staring at him, ghosting the doorframe of her living room, she realized that no matter how hard she tried to push him away now, it would ultimately fail.

He was a part of her life no matter which way she turned.

CHAPTER SIX

Church on Sunday morning was thankfully warm. The freezing rain and plummeting temperatures had stretched on for days, never once letting up. It was a welcoming sight to see the sky and bright sun for the first time since the colder temperatures. The land was still wet from the rain, and flowers drooped over in their flowerbeds in shock from the cold. The community gathered outside after one last hymn was sung and eagerly enjoyed the warm air before it disappeared again. Another storm lipped the horizon, the clouds brewing above the mountain tops.

Matilda titled her head to smile and welcome the warm sun. She sat on the blanket that Rosella had spread out for them on a patch of grass so they could sit together while they ate, but her *kinner* had already left to talk and play with their friends. She didn't mind the temporary peace. Since the accident, her *kinner* barely left her side, so she welcomed the quiet to reflect.

It was the first day that her side did not throb from the stitches. Bishop Abraham had dedicated their morning prayers to Matilda's recovery, and she marveled at the after affects. The constant ache in her side had faded away as though *Gott's* fingers had been there, carefully mending the wounded flesh. Thankfully, her non-stop headache had passed finally two days prior, and her vision had finally cleared as well.

"Danka Gott," she whispered, closing her eyes. She kept her thoughts on *Gott* and Him alone, allowing her mind to be full of praise for all that He had done for her.

Footsteps alerted her that someone was approaching, and she straightened from where she had been leaning back on her hands. When she opened her eyes, she saw Eli striding towards her. The pit of her stomach tightened defensively as it always did now whenever she caught sight of Eli's gaze on her. After Rosella mentioned that Betty had overheard him talking to their Bishop about her relationship with Ryan, she felt a growing unease around Eli. She certainly didn't want to add to his hope that courtship might still be in the future.

"How are you feeling?" he asked, concern showing in his face and voice. "Your *maemm* told me you would be at home resting for a while. I've been meaning to come visit you, but…."

His hazel eyes sparkled as he crouched easily on his heels, hands draped loosely on his thighs. The scent of fresh mountain air and soap washed over her when a breeze stirred the strands of his beard. She did appreciate his genuine concern for her well-being and pulled her dress closer to give him more room.

"I'm doing better, *danka,*" she said, offering him a small smile. "I was at home resting for a little bit, but I plan to be back at work tomorrow."

"That's *gut.* I am glad you are feeling better. I was worried about you, but I wasn't sure if you would like company or not."

At his words, an awkward silence fell between them.

Matilda toyed with a few pulled threads on the edge of the blanket, debating on whether to invite Eli to join her. She gave a silent prayer asking *Gott* to help her decide, then caught sight of Ryan standing with a group of *mensleit* near the barn. He had turned his body so that he could watch them. He stood, hands shoved deeply into his trouser pockets, and scowled before he turned his attention back to the group.

Could he truly be jealous of Eli? It seemed a bit absurd given that they had barely spoken since her crash.

Eli had apparently also watched their exchange as she felt him tense as he turned back to her. Unease, distrust, she wasn't sure what he was feeling but his emotions played across his face. He worked his jaw a few times as though fighting an urge to say something but his customary resistance won out.

She decided to get whatever was going on out into the open. "Do you want to say something?"

Eli shifted and looked off into the distance. "I wish you would be careful around him."

"Around who?"

"You know who I am talking about."

He looked back at her with a deep sadness as he shook his head and sighed. "I'm only trying to —"

"Protect me?" Matilda finished for him. "You're only trying to protect me? How can you say such things, Eli? I wouldn't be here if it wasn't for him, or at the least I'd be seriously injured. He is a part of our community and a *gut* man."

Eli refused to back down. "I realize that he saved you from further sickness and injury. For that, everyone is grateful. It's not that I speak of; it's the way he looks at you, Matilda. It's not right. Temptation is written all over his face."

Matilda felt a hot flush spread up the sides of her neck. She wasn't sure whether it was from anger, or from hearing how Ryan looked at her but the heat came from within and couldn't be denied. "Are you implying that he is not a godly man?"

"Of course he's not," Eli said and stood his ground. "Ryan Myers is not a part of our community, nor did he grow up with our shared morals and faith. He is in the time of testing and as far as I've seen, failing at it miserably."

She lowered her gaze to hide the wince from Eli's well-placed hit. She had a brief thought that she could maybe change his mind if he she shared the truth with him. That even they, those in her Amish community, could make mistakes despite all their foundation in the faith. They were by no means perfect when it came to resisting temptations, something she'd come to realize at sixteen when she gave in to temptation. But Samuel believed as she that the good *Gott* in His mercy forgives and allows for his children to return to Him and lead a *gut* life. *Gott* knows she did her level best.

Eli continued, his voice dropping lower. "Do you honestly think he will continue to be here? He barely coped with the weather, and I have seen his forward behavior when interacting with the females within the community. It is not *gut*. There is trouble written all over him. Why can't you see it?"

"*Gott* has a plan for each one of us, Eli. Ryan has every right to be here, as much as we do. The Bishop, the community, we all accepted him for this year of trials and tests. He comes to me for spiritual help. What would you like me to do? Ignore him? Run away, maybe to you?"

Matilda stopped at her rush of words and they hung in the air like so many shirts clipped to a clothesline. A part of her was appalled at what she'd said, but another, deeper, more hurt part felt justified. Why couldn't Eli acknowledge that perhaps *Gott* had a hand in all this?

Instead, Eli said, "My offer of courtship and marriage still stands."

Matilda closed her eyes in chagrin. Her last question had flown out of her in frustration, but she hadn't expected an answer, especially this one. She had prayed hard over their situation, but firmly believed that *Gott* would have brought them together if it was meant to be. Eli was by all means a *gut mann*, but from the depths of her heart she honestly didn't believe *Gott* intended for her to marry Eli. With that deep confirmation, Matilda opened her eyes and met his waiting hazel ones.

She tried to pick her words carefully. After all, Eli had been a *gut* friend and they shared a common bond of the death of spouse. "I've already told you, Eli. The answer is *nee*. You and I both know that this isn't right."

Despite his best efforts, Eli's face revealed the pain of her words and his body rocked backward. "I don't believe that, Matilda. There is something else holding you back. Something with Ryan, though you deny it. Perhaps even he doesn't know."

Matilda's calm demeanor felt a hit from Eli's sharp observation. Unable to meet his stare any longer, Matilda smoothed the skirts of her blue dress around her knees as she got ready to rise. "I don't know what you mean. I'm not hiding anything."

She got to her feet rather unsteadily and Eli reached to help but she managed to make it without his assistance. She had to wait for him to fully stand before she could hide behind the business of snatching the blanket from the ground and shaking it free of grass. She was done with the conversation and hoped Eli would finally understand. Clouds had once again gathered above them and the sunlight faded, leaving a coolness similar to the one between them. The air was damp with the promise of another cold rain.

The last thing she wanted for herself or Mathew was to be caught in the rain. She turned away from Eli to search for Isaac and Matthew in the hay field alongside the barn. She spotted them jogging happily along with the other *kinner* as they laughed at something before taking in the smiling faces of her community. After a few minutes, she realized that Rosella's familiar face didn't readily appear.

"Excuse me, Eli. I must go find Rosella — "

"Wait."

Eli grabbed hold of her elbow. Their eyes met and this time his tone was apologetic. "I'm sorry. Whatever is going on is not my business, nor do I have the right to make assumptions. I pray every day for *Gott* to help me not judge others, but I can't help it sometimes when it comes to him."

Matilda gave him the moment. "Do you think I cannot see your concerns? I understand them, but you're also implying that I cannot resist him. My faith is stronger than you think."

Gently prying his fingers from her elbow, Matilda brushed past him before anything else could be said. Tears wetted her lashes, and she discreetly wiped them with the back of her hand as she charged on. Her faith hadn't been as strong at sixteen, but time had changed that as it naturally changed the world. Today, she could resist Ryan if it were to ever go to that point again. With *Gott's* help and will, she knew it was true.

Matilda looked up from the ground as she walked towards the barn, meeting Ryan's gaze in the process. She suspected that he had observed them the entire time from the way he glanced between her and Eli who had remained in the same spot.

She then did something that she didn't expect and certainly surprised Ryan.

It was an impulsive action, but she reached out to brush his shoulder as she passed by. That briefest of touch had her heart racing with a realization.

Perhaps Eli was right. She would not be able to resist Ryan.

Several days passed and Wednesday offered up a wonderful day. For her lunch break, Matilda took advantage of the nice afternoon weather to walk to Samuel's old buggy repair shop.

Not Samuel's buggy repair shop, she reminded herself firmly. It was now Jacob's buggy repair shop, and Ryan had graciously taken her buggy in to be fixed for free of charge. He had left word at the bakery yesterday with her *maemm* that the repairs would be finished by the afternoon.

They had yet to talk to one another since the accident, and Matilda felt a certain excitement as she wondered how their next interaction would go. Her dream of Samuel still lingered within her heart, tugging at her rather harshly at times. She found it hard to decipher. Had he truly been him giving her permission to let go or was it her mind filling in the answer?

Matilda enjoyed her time outside as the sidewalks were empty other than the few window-shopping tourists who strolled down Main Street. She kept her gaze down on the concrete to avoid conversation. With each step closer to the shop, her courage wavered. Her pace slowed until she finally stepped onto the gravel parking lot in front of the repair shop and stopped.

The repair shop was even tidier than she remembered. A couple of black buggies were parked squarely in front of the shop for all to see. The front door was propped open with a large rock, and she could hear the distant *clink* of a hammer hitting a nail and echoing through the afternoon air. The sun relentlessly bored down as she looked around.

So hot, she thought, as she fanned her face and dabbed at the sweat.

Her mood had changed now that she faced the shop and memories of Samuel. Maybe she should have waited and simply had Ryan drop off the buggy. After all, she could always use her parent's spare buggy until then.

"Matilda?"

Lost in second thoughts, Matilda started in surprise at the voice behind her and turned.

"Jacob." Matilda breathed out and placed her hand over her fast-beating heart. "You snuck up on me. I didn't even hear you approach."

Jacob adjusted his hat and seemed equally as startled. Oil stains coated his brown button-down shirt, and wood shavings covered his pant legs. "I didn't mean to sneak up on you," he said. "I'm surprised to see you here."

"I thought I'd stop by, say hello, see how you're doing...."

She trailed off as Jacob stared at her in bewilderment. What was her problem, she wondered. Jacob knew as well as she did that she avoided the buggy repair shop since Samuel's death and this would only be the second time she'd stopped by.

"I'm sorry," she said, pinching the bridge of her nose. "I know I haven't been around since Samuel died, yet here I am. Crazy, right?"

Jacob gave her a soft smile. "*Nee*. I don't think so, but you could just say that you are here to pick up the buggy Ryan repaired. To make it simple for you."

Matilda smiled thankfully at Jacob's understanding. He had always been so sensitive to others' feelings, and had given her plenty of space to grieve after Samuel died. He didn't seek her out at church to inquire how she was or stop by the bakery. Jacob and Samuel had been close friends for such a long time and even looked similar to one another from the same hair color to the light-hearted jokes. He knew that he represented a painful part of her past as Samuel's best friend.

"*Danka,* Jacob. It's hard being here."

"I understand. Let's get your buggy." He flourished a tanned arm in the direction of the buggy shop and followed behind her as they walked together across the gravel.

"Tell me," he asked. "How are you feeling?" He matched his stride to hers as they walked, his hands plunged into his trouser pockets. "I heard about the crash, and judging from the condition your buggy was in, it was a bad one."

Matilda tried to ignore the sudden rush of chills cascading through her body at the thought of that night. She truly had been blessed by *Gott's* protection. "I am *gut* now that I no longer have a headache or stitches to worry about."

Jacob nodded emphatically. "I know how that feels. Remember when I was kicked in the head by that horse Samuel brought with him from Lancaster? I hated every second that I had those stitches on my forehead."

Matilda smiled wistfully as she glanced at the faint scar along his smooth forehead. He hadn't changed all that much. They had brought very little from Lancaster back then, but Samuel adamantly refused to leave behind his horse, Mary. It took several months for them to save enough money to have Mary transported to Colorado. Matilda had a suspicion that Samuel's parents had paid for half of the transportation costs. The fiery red horse's temperament quickly earned her the name "Feisty Mary." Only Samuel had been able to ride her. Everyone else, she either kicked or nipped.

Matilda grinned. "I remember you cursing loudly at Mary for hours when you were trying to get her into the pen."

"That horse was a nightmare. I still don't understand why he loved that horse as much as he did."

"Ha!" she said, laughing. "I sometimes had the suspicion that he loved Mary more than he loved me or the *kinner*."

Once they reached the workshop area, Jacob bent down to grab the door firmly in both hands before shoving it upwards. Sawdust swirled along the concrete floor from the breeze and tickled her nose while the soothing smell of wood filled her lungs. She breathed in the scent. Samuel had always smelt of wood and fresh air. She remembered how, even in the midst of all shop work, she couldn't ever recall a time he looked disheveled.

A buggy, freshly sanded with a new carriage, wheels, and axels, sat in the middle of the shop. She dimly remembered the mangled wood and shattered carriage as she was being lifted into another buggy. There was no way this was the same buggy.

Matilda swallowed thickly at the sight and turned to Jacob. "Where is my buggy?"

"Outside," Ryan's voice answered from within the shop before Jacob could answer.

Ryan appeared from behind shelves of spare buggy parts, wiping his hands clean from oil. Their eyes met and that brief interaction left Matilda's skin prickling from the sensation of butterflies in the pit of her stomach. She shifted her attention to the newly constructed buggy before she lost track of all rational thought.

"This looks brand new. You didn't have to build me a new one," Matilda said, marveling at the new buggy yet feeling a bit overwhelmed.

"You're right, I didn't have to," Ryan said, coming to stand besides the main carriage. "But you needed one given the crumpled mess of your buggy after the accident."

Matilda's aversion to the new buggy sprung from several sources, including a big financial one. "I cannot pay for this, Ryan. I don't have the money for a whole new buggy."

Ryan leaned back against the buggy door and smiled a small, ghostly smile. "Consider it a token of gratitude for helping me out all these months."

Matilda felt a barrage of opposition surge forward and opened her mouth to retort, but then clicked her jaw shut. No use in arguing with Ryan in front of Jacob who was already watching their exchange with a bit more curiosity than she liked. Maybe Jacob thought Ryan was making a friendly gesture, but she knew him well enough to know that simply wasn't true. Ryan might be dressed in Amish clothes and ways, but he remained a business man. He had to expect some kind of payment.

"You didn't have to do this," she replied. "A simple *danka* would have been enough."

The sound of horse hooves crunching on the gravel filled the shop and put their conversation on pause. Jacob smiled briefly before excusing himself to see who had arrived. The second Jacob was out of ear shot, Matilda took a step forward, braced her hands firmly on the opposite buggy door, and kept her voice low. "What is wrong with you? You can't just hand out free buggies."

"I don't hand out free buggies."

"I must pay for this."

Ryan let out a huge, exaggerated sigh and shook his head in wry amusement. "You really don't make anything easy, do you Mattie?"

Matilda refused to let his attitude get in the way. "I'm being serious. How much is this new buggy?"

"For you? Free. Of course, we could throw in you spending a Saturday night with me, but I guess that will depend on how nice you are going to be about this."

She knew he was baiting her and evidently enjoying every minute of it. Matilda huffed angrily, determined not to fall to his charms. "You're impossible sometimes. Do you know that?"

"Only sometimes?" Ryan met her angry stare with a big grin. "Relax, Mattie. I helped Jacob figure some things out for the shop business-wise and so we worked out this exchange. You honestly needed a new buggy."

Matilda didn't know what to do. *Gott* knew her need and had more than met it with this brand new buggy, but she felt it was way more than she needed. She didn't want to stand out amongst the community with a brand new carriage, especially one offered by Ryan. There was enough talk. "You make everything complicated by doing things like this. You still don't get —"

The buggy shifted beneath her hands suddenly. Ryan leaped onto the buggy step, and leaned forward to catch her hand in his. Before she could tug away, he pressed a warm kiss to the back of her hand.

Heat met her skin and a fire coursed through her veins at the touch of his lips. It paralyzed her in the way he knew it would. He cradled her much smaller hand between his, holding it tightly.

"I'm happy that you are okay, Mattie. You honestly have no idea how scary that was for me when I found you."

"Ryan —"

He pressed his lips again to her fingers and quieted her protests once more. "Stop fighting the inevitable, Mattie. Aren't you getting tired of it?"

"I —" Matilda's eyes closed, and she couldn't stop the sigh of pleasure as Ryan's fingers traced the outline of her hand. "Yes, I am tired —."

"*Gut*. I am too."

CHAPTER SEVEN

Where are we going again?" Rosella said, her voice fueled by the surly teenager tone that constantly tried Matilda's patience.

Matilda turned to look over her shoulder at Rosella. Her *kinner* were seated in the back of the market wagon, their legs dangling off the edge as they took in their surroundings. Rosella, too, had twisted around to look up at them. Thick forest foliage, green and wet from yesterday's rainfall, crowded around the winding mountain road. After a week of cold rain, a warm Saturday afternoon felt too special not to enjoy, and Ryan had insisted they accompany him on a ride.

He sat next to Matilda, his long legs bent at the knees with the leather reins held firmly in his hand. Today, he wore a straw hat that shaded his face from the sunlight, and a maroon button-down shirt that needed to be patched at the elbows. Whenever the wagon's wheels hit a hole or rock, the motion caused the sides of their legs to brush briefly before Matilda would try her best to scoot away. She didn't wish to have her *kinner*, who had finally started to accept Ryan since the buggy accident, see them touching even if it was unintentional.

Ryan smiled at Rosella's questions. "To a lake that I found a few weekends ago," he answered. "Don't worry. You'll love it."

The answering look on Rosella's face suggested otherwise but to her credit she kept her mouth wisely closed.

"Are we going fishing?" Matthew asked.

Isaac intercepted Ryan's answer, eagerly asking, "Can we please go fishing, Ma? Then, we can have it for dinner."

Matilda smiled at Isaac's beaming face. "If we are fishing, *ja*, then we can have fish for dinner," she said, giving Ryan a wordless question. When he nodded his agreement, she relaxed back against the wooden seat.

Sunlight shimmered through the leafy tops as the wagon continued to lumber up the mountainside that smelt of fresh rain. Matilda kept her gaze on the patches of sunshine and tried not think of the dream she had after the buggy accident. For an irrational moment, she thought of telling Ryan that they had to return home. Going close to *Gott's* creation was what Samuel, her, and the *kinner* had done whenever they needed to be close to one another and to *Gott*. How would Samuel feel to know that Ryan was replacing his spot within their family?

Except Ryan wasn't replacing Samuel's spot.

She reminded herself firmly of this when Ryan also tilted his head up to look at the sunshine. The bits of sunlight that leaked through the tree tops reflected on his cheekbones, and close as she was to him, she could see the almost-green specks in the depths of his cerulean blue eyes. Matilda turned to glance at Rosella, her oldest, as she sported a smile and studied the surrounding forest. When Rosella gave her a curious look, Matilda took advantage of the moment to stare into her familiar eyes. Rosella had the same green specks.

Matilda felt a tightness in her stomach as she tried to swallow. She knew it was merely a matter of time before her secret would surface, whether she gave it up due to a breakdown in nerves, or whether she took control and confessed the truth to Ryan. Either way, his reaction would not be pleasant; nor would Rosella's.

As he pulled on the reins for the horse to stop, Ryan gave out a hearty, "Here we are." When he turned to her and her *kinner*, he had such a boyish, goofy grin on his face. "Hop out all of you. I promise that you will like what you're about to see."

The road continued upwards at a sharp incline, too steep for the wagon to continue upwards without anyone falling out. The grass surrounding the road was tangled and filled with various wild flowers of shades of purple and red that somehow had survived the bouts of cold. Patches of snow spotted the forest floor, protected by the shade of the tall pine trees.

"Where are we?" Isaac asked, twisting his body to look at Ryan in confusion. "I've never been up here before."

Ryan walked around the wagon to help Rosella jump out, and then went to Matilda. He stretched up a hand, but his fair head was turned to her *kinner* who were staring at the wild foliage. Matilda slipped a hand into his much stronger one, and stepped down easily into a ditch filled with overgrown weeds. Her heart jumped at Ryan's simple touch, and she let go before the compulsion to hold his hand became too hard to resist. The smell of damp earth and pine filled the mountain air. Underneath the shade of the trees a much cooler air touched the back of her neck, and she folded her arms to suppress a shiver.

"I don't get what we are looking at," Rosella said, placing a hand on Matthew's shoulder as they peered. "Are we here just to look at flowers? Or, what?"

"The surprise isn't here," Ryan replied. He grabbed the wicker basket Matilda had packed full with sandwiches and various cheeses from where it had been strapped down and pointed forward. "We have to hike through there for about a mile or so."

They all looked at him in apprehension. The path on the opposite side of the road had been clearly made from someone walking through the calf-high grass. Matilda felt a growing unease as her gaze followed the path deep into the forest.

"I don't know about this, Ryan. That path goes straight into the forest and," she paused, taking the basket Ryan offered and looping one of her elbows through the handle, "it's the springtime. Bears are starting to wake from hibernation, and we can't bring the buggy through there so we have to leave the horse here."

You think that path was made by some strange person?" Ryan asked, seeming unconcerned with her doubts. He reached into a chest behind the front seat of the wagon and pulled out a shotgun in a leather holster. "Not to worry, Mattie. We're safe. Try not to worry so much about everything. We're here for to give you and your *kinner* a chance to relax."

Matilda eyed the shotgun, the path, and the shotgun again. "Not sure I can relax knowing you have a shotgun. Have you ever handled a gun?"

Ryan gave her what she assumed was his attempt at a comforting grin. "For a long time, actually. I've had this gun all along in case there were attacks against the live-stock, and I'm no stranger to firearms. Maybe I didn't strike you as the type to know anything about real life out here, but we did only know each other for a couple of months and that was a long time ago. I would hope, Mattie, that you'd trust me with your and your *kinner's* pro-tection."

"Hold this," he said to her, as he handed over the shot-gun and ignored her glare from the use of her nickname. "We won't be leaving the horse."

Cradling the rather heavy shotgun in her arms, Matilda felt eyes upon her and turned to look at Rosella who promptly looked away. She knew her daughter, who didn't miss anything, had caught the use of her nickname again. There was sure to be fallout.

Ryan unbuckled his horse from the wagon and gathered the reins in his hand. He took back his shotgun, and with the barrel resting against his shoulder, marched through the underbrush. Her two sons followed behind him with-out question, their curiosity officially captured by Ryan's surprise. Rosella slowly turned on her heel after staring at Matilda, and hitched up the skirts of her dress to keep them from getting snagged in twigs.

Matilda stepped over a rotting log scaring off a skink or two and followed behind them. It seemed like the pathway stretched on forever with Ryan at front, leading the horse, and them, through the forest. Clusters of trees including poplars and magnolias stood together as they passed be-neath shadows, and the distinct smell from the evergreen pines filled Matilda's lungs pleasantly as they walked along the rugged terrain. Her sons' voices echoed in the still air as they danced happily through the wild grass, and chatted happily with Ryan who smiled patiently as they rambled on and on about various topics. While she was tense with anxiety, her heart warmed at the sight of her sons talking with Ryan as if they had known them their entire lives. It was something that Eli had tried hard to achieve, but couldn't succeed in. The only one who remained distant was Rosella, but even then Matilda caught a small smile gracing Rosella's face at some humorous reply Ryan had made.

Maybe it wouldn't be so bad having Ryan be a part of their lives. Her *kinner* didn't seem to mind having him around them. He was slowly starting to fit into their community and break down their protective walls. It was so tempting, she thought, to give in to the feelings that were bubbling beneath the surface. Yet, she also knew more closeness yielded greater risk that her secret would be exposed.

All those thoughts faded away the moment they emerged from the forest, and Ryan's surprise unfolded itself in front of their eyes.

The small valley was filled with columbines of various colors from magenta to solid blue, and evergreen trees that circled the small crystalline lake that sat in the middle. Sunlight glimmered off the smooth surface, but what drew Matilda's attention was the group of white swans swimming peacefully together. Her footsteps drew her closer to the water's edge where her *kinner* also had gathered to peer at the swans with eager curiosity.

"They're beautiful," Rosella said, speaking in a low, breathy voice. So beautiful."

Ryan appeared at Matilda's side and stared at the two white beauties as well, though he also sported a big smile. He turned to look at the four of them as he, too, spoke softly, "We have to be very quiet. They have excellent hearing and their vision is darn good, too."

The boys crouched lower and silently shushed each other.

"I found them when I was up here the other day to pray," Ryan continued. "Do you see those two swans over there?" He pointed across the lake to two white swans, their necks arched elegantly to form the shape of a heart. "They are called courting mute swans, and they mate only for life, unlike other birds who have different partners every season. They stick with each other all year around, raising baby swans, and they are the fiercest birds to face if their loved one is under attack. They are much stronger than what their beauty and grace suggests."

Enthralled with them, Matilda stepped a little closer until the lake's water lapped gently at the toes of her shoes. She marveled at the pure whiteness of their feathers, as they glided gracefully along the water's surface. She found herself in reverence to such a beautiful image and creation from *Gott*. Deeper than that, she found herself in awe to know that such beautiful creatures carried the same sense of faith and beliefs when it came to love as the Amish did.

Mathew cocked his head and frowned, still staying low and out of sight. "They don't look as if they are strong." He looked up at Ryan. "What would happen if you go near them?"

"I wouldn't suggest doing it," Ryan said, shaking his head. "Swans like these have been rumored to break bones and cause some mean cuts. Look here."

Matilda reluctantly looked over to see Ryan rolling up the sleeve of his shirt to show them a white bandage wrapped tightly around his forearm. "This," he said, tapping the bandage, "is a wound that needed four stitches. I tried to approach one of the female swans, and her mate decided to give me a warning bite."

Isaac's eyes grew wide. "A swan did that?" When he looked at the swans again he seemed to have new respect for these creatures of *Gott*. "Maybe we should leave, maybe go somewhere else? What if they were to come over here or — "

"Don't worry. They won't bother you if you don't bother them," Ryan said, rolling his sleeve back down. "I've been up here for hours at a time, and they haven't come near me."

Isaac and Matthew exchanged uneasy looks, but shrugged before they picked their way from where the swan's patrolled the shoreline and wandered further down to search for rocks to skim along the lake's surface. Meanwhile, with Rosella's help, Matilda grabbed a quilted blanket to lay across a dry patch of grass that was far away from the tree line and the cool shade.

Rosella wandered over to Ryan who stood nearby but still watched the swans. "Are there more swans around here?" Rosella asked, as she eyed the lake's distant shore.

Ryan nodded. "A few, but I'm not here all the time, so I don't know if they are all here during the day."

Matilda busied herself with lunch but she could hear their small talk and was happy that Rosella was making an effort to be nice to Ryan.

"I'm going to get closer to them. If I'm really quiet and cautious, do you really think they'd attack me?" Rosella asked.

"I don't think that's the best idea, Rosella." Matilda started, but Ryan hushed her concerns.

"Just don't get too close," he said. "Stay clear of the water's edge."

Matilda and Ryan watched Rosella creep around the lake shore to get closer to the swans. When she neared Matthew and Isaac, she clearly paused to dissuade them from throwing any more stones into the lake. Finally, unable to resist the warmth of the sunlight, Matilda eased down on the blanket and adjusted the skirts of her gray dress to cover her legs appropriately.

"So..." Ryan said, sitting down next to her. "What do you think about the swans?"

"They are beautiful birds. I've never seen any until now. Only heard of them mentioned once or twice."

"Not even in Lancaster?"

Matilda shook her head negatively. The two sat side by side with their arms wrapped loosely around their bent knees. The hair on Ryan's arm tickled the backside of her hand when he shifted next to her to get comfortable.

"I've always loved swans. There was a park near my mom's house, and mute swans used to go there all the time. We would walk to the park to watch them and feed them pieces of bread. They say that in some branches of

Christianity the swan is symbolic of grace and purity while in other branches they see swans as a sign of evil."

"Evil?" Matilda echoed, fascinated with this knowledge. She stared out at the pure white birds. "How could anyone think that those creatures are evil? They are *Gott's* creation."

Ryan shrugged. "Some swans have black underneath them. I guess some believe they portray themselves as pure when they actually aren't."

"But they are pure though," Matilda argued. "As you said, they mate only for life."

A smile tugged at the corner of his lips. "You love the swans as much as I do. Go figure. I finally managed to get you to hang out with me without you throwing excuses about how we cannot, should not, would not."

"Don't get any ideas," Matilda said, and lifted her gaze upwards. "Besides, my *kinner* are here. You're starting to win them over, by the way. Not even —"

Matilda paused when that realization sunk in even further beyond words. Not even Eli could win her *kinner's* trust, but somehow Ryan had managed to do so and in a short time, too. She shook her head in surprise.

"Not even Eli?" Ryan said, finishing her sentence. "Eli, the other courter?"

Unable to resist, Matilda gave him a playful smack on the shoulder. "He is not the other courter. At some point he might have gotten the idea that we could be together, but it wasn't right. It wasn't *Gott's* will."

"Are you sure about that?" Ryan asked, still smiling but with an edge to his voice. "He's given me the impression that he thinks otherwise."

Matilda wondered if she heard an undercurrent of jealousy. When Ryan turned away to look absently in another direction, she knew and she grinned. "You're jealous!" she said, poking him in the shoulder. "I saw it. You're jealous of Eli."

Ryan continued to look away. "I'm merely concerned with the fact that he seems to think you will marry him someday."

"I'm pretty sure that's what jealousy means."

Ryan didn't get a chance to respond. A loud wailing filled the air when a rock soared particularly close to the area where a lone swan swam peacefully. The bird fluttered and set its sights on the two boys and swam toward a guilty-looking Matthew and Isaac, who both stood with stones still clutched in their hands.

"*Maemm!*" Rosella yelled, pointing to her *bruders* with an accusing finger. "They are throwing rocks at the swans."

The stones dropped to the ground. Matthew and Isaac backed up nervously as the swan came to a stop a few feet away from the shore line and gave another loud wail.

"We didn't mean to get that close," Isaac said.

"It was honestly a mistake," Matthew chimed in.

Rosella glared at them both. "It wasn't a mistake. I watched them aim right at the swans."

Before the argument could escalate, Matilda waved the three of them over. "No more throwing stones. Come over here and eat some lunch."

The boys trudged over to the blanket. Matilda could see that they both wanted to continue to play by the lake.

"But what are we going to do all day here?" Isaac asked, plopping down in front of Ryan. "I don't want to stare at swans all day. I mean, they are pretty but, well, there must be more to do? Can we throw rocks some more?"

"The swans don't bother me," Rosella said. "I love them."

"*Gut* thing I brought some extra fishing poles," Ryan said. He grinned when Matthew and Isaac cheered happily at the news.

They all quickly finished their ham and cheddar cheese sandwiches on fresh white bread. While Ryan helped Matthew and Isaac with their fishing poles, Matilda and Rosella cleaned up the blanket.

"He's not so bad, you know?" Rosella said, her voice casual as she swept away a few crumbs from the blanket, while looking in Ryan's direction. "I mean, he's not *daed*, or anything, but I like him for the most part."

Matilda's heart flipped at Rosella's confession. She nearly blurted out everything at her daughter's words. It all bubbled and roiled beneath the surface of her skin, always promising to erupt. Her stomach gave a sharp twist, a bodily reminder. The closer she and her *kinner* grew to Ryan, the closer her long-held secret would be no more.

Her terrified musing was interrupted when Ryan held out a fishing pole for Rosella to use. With her *kinner* happily occupied, chatting among one another, Ryan finally motioned for Matilda to follow him into a cluster of trees. Matilda tried to ignore the loud pounding of her heart as she followed his tall frame into the wooded area. While they were hidden from her *kinner's* eyes thanks to the canopy overhead, Matilda could watch them perfectly through the foliage and branches.

"I wanted to show you something else as well," Ryan admitted as he stepped off to the side to reveal a patch of white flowers with large petals surrounded by green grass and various columbines. Sunlight shimmered down from the treetops, reflecting off the drops of water on the petals as they trailed down into the center of the flower. "I've never seen flowers like these before. Don't even know what their name is."

Matilda stepped forward to have a better look. "I've never seen them before either," she whispered, amazed that one more of *Gott's* pure white creations had been revealed. She smiled, touched by such a simple gesture. "*Danka* for today. The swans, these flowers… It has really brightened our day."

"You're welcome. Here," he said and bent down to pluck a flower free before taking another step toward her. Matilda swallowed as his fingers brushed against the side of her cheek when he tucked the stem of the flower beneath her *kapp* and ear. "They remind me of you."

Her heart hammered. A strong hand cupped the side of her neck, his thumb brushing intimately over her rapidly beating pulse. Every instinct screamed at her to pull away, to tell him that this was beyond proper, but in an instant she was sixteen years old again, and felt the same way as when their lips meet in that first kiss that had Matilda's knees trembling.

"*Maemm?*"

A bucket of ice tumbled down upon Matilda's head. She jerked back from Ryan, her lips still moist and tingling from their brief kiss. Twigs snapped behind them, signaling that one of her *kinner* was coming to search for them. Matilda disentangled herself from Ryan's grip right as Matthew stepped into the clearing with fishing pole in hand. He held up a rainbow trout in triumph to show them. "I caught the first fish! Can we have him for dinner?"

"*Ja,*" Matilda said. "Let's clean him up, and keep him cold until we leave." Thanking *Gott* that, by some miracle, her voice didn't shake like the rest of her did.

She placed a hand on Matthew's shoulder and led him out back to the lake without sparing one glance in Ryan's direction. If she did, *Gott* knew she would give into the frightening temptation flowing through her.

Some part of her had hoped that maybe the tension between them would ease up with this one kiss. What was she thinking? Instead, it made her want him even more, and that thought alone left her plotting for a way to put distance between them. Even if it would only end in futile hope.

CHAPTER EIGHT

A thunderstorm brewed in the sky above the Sangre de Cristo mountain range a few days later. The air was thick with the promise of rain that would most likely downpour at the first boom of thunder. Matilda kept the back door of the bakery propped open to allow the fresh and cooler air in, but also to listen for Lily's return from the local grocery store.

She added powdered sugar and a tablespoon of vanilla to the boiling peanut butter mixture before pouring the mixture over the cooling sheet cake. Her stomach grumbled in anticipation when she thought of having a slice later at her parent's *haus* while celebrating Lily's sixteenth birthday. Up front, Rebecca kept busy by helping customers, and giving Matilda the time to bake the peanut butter sheet cake, a big part of their family tradition. She couldn't recall a time that her *maemm* had ever made a different cake for any of their birthdays.

Matilda picked up a spatula and smoothed the frosting over the moist top of the cake. Lost in her thoughts, she jumped when a sudden knock on the back door echoed in the silent kitchen.

In came Ryan, who stood in the doorway slightly hunched at the shoulders to avoid hitting the top of his head on the door frame. He smiled warmly as he reached up to pull off his straw hat. Just the sight of him alone dressed in a dark blue button-down shirt and dust-covered pant legs sent her heart racing. Their short kiss at the lake replayed in her mind and teased her constantly. When her lips started to tingle at the thought, she bit down on her lips to stop the sensation — and the temptation. They had been in privacy then, and she certainly didn't wish to risk Rebecca stumbling upon them.

The mere thought of Rebecca's response made her pause. What a scene that would be, she thought, and placed the spatula in a bowl she had used earlier. She smiled at Ryan, albeit shyly.

"*Gut* morning," he said and stepped into the kitchen. He sniffed the air appreciatively for a few seconds, "Is that a peanut butter cake I smell?"

"*Ja.* My sister's birthday is today, and peanut butter cake is what my family uses to celebrate birthdays."

"No kidding?" He looked down at the large sheet of cake with a wistful smile. "My mom used to bake a mean peanut butter cake for my birthday, too. Nothing beats creamy peanut butter. Remind me to ask for this cake on my birthday, especially since you know how to bake one."

"I will," she said, smiling. "What are you doing here so early?"

Ryan shrugged his shoulders. He picked up the spatula she had placed in the bowl and wiped a finger along it to gather the last bit of frosting left. "We're caught up with work, and there's nothing for me to fix today, so I thought I would come by and see you before I went in."

Her heart thumped in pleasure but maybe with anticipation, too. She felt her cheeks flame hot and knew they displayed her response. She ducked her head down to hide the shy smile forming. When she finally glanced at him, she found him standing there with his eyes closed and a very pleased smile on his face. When he finally opened his eyes, he almost beamed, and she couldn't help but notice a slight bit of peanut butter frosting on his lower lip.

"I think," he said, "you are one of the best bakers in this country. You should open up your own shop."

High praise coming from Ryan as she knew how critical he could be when it came to business. "This shop will be mine once my *maemm* can't continue working," she said, excited at the thought. "My *maemm* does the business parts of running it since I am hopeless when it comes to things like that. I'm just *gut* at baking and dealing with customers."

Matilda resumed frosting the sheet cake as Ryan walked around the kitchen looking at the minimal amount of equipment used to run the bakery. "You're in luck," he said. "I happen to be a pretty savvy business person, and I could teach you everything you need to know. After all, you've taught me quite a few things."

She looked at him in surprise but continued smoothing a few patches here and there on the cake. "Not that much. You've learned a lot from the *mensleit*. I only taught you a couple of common phrases."

Ryan turned his attention back to her. "I wasn't talking about that. I was talking about having faith in *Gott* no matter what. Not everybody can have that much faith in *Gott* as you do."

At his word, she shook her head no but said, "What would our world be without *Gott* in it?"

"I'd say chaotic and filled with constant headaches — and I should know."

Matilda bit the inside of her lip to keep herself from smiling foolishly. The jittery feeling intensified when Ryan tilted his head to the side and studied her. With him standing in the kitchen with her, she couldn't help but wonder how it would feel to have him at her side, helping her run the bakery with business skills.

"So, how does this work?" He asked suddenly, breaking her reverie.

"How does what work?"

"You know, dating. Or," he paused, frowning slightly in thought, "I think you called it courtship, so guess I mean courtship. How does that whole thing work for the Amish? I never really asked anyone."

Matilda stopped focusing on the cake and her sister's impending celebration. She stopped thinking about the bakery and her future. Matilda stopped thinking at all. Courtship? A burst of images flamed across her mind and her skin responded with an equal amount of heat. She'd be lying to herself but even more to *Gott* if she pretended it had never crossed her mind. When she was sixteen and on Rumspringa, the thought had totally occupied her mind as she tried to imagine Ryan within her Amish family and community. Ryan, dressed in Plain clothes and following the *Ordnung*. Back then she'd easily found the strength to push those images aside. Now some of those silly daydreams had become a reality, they weren't so easy to ignore. A wave of intense fear crashed down upon her. Emotions flooded her. She didn't know what to feel.

"Mattie?"

Ryan's voice broke through the barrage of emotions and drew her back to the present. "I'm sorry," she said, wishing for a fast comeback. "I was thinking about something." She pinched the bridge of her nose, still unable to control her surging emotions. "I'll have to explain courting to you later. I have to finish frosting this cake before Lily returns and must get back to baking some pies."

She saw Ryan's confusion at her sudden change of mood but she couldn't help him right now. He was about to say something, but Rebecca entered the kitchen and smiled them both. "*Ach*, I'm sorry. I didn't realize you were here, Ryan."

Ryan seemed to recover just fine. "I was just stopping by on my way to work."

Rebecca nodded. "I've been hearing *gut* things about you at the buggy shop. Jacob swears that you have brought in more money to help with the community and with the business."

"I merely showed him a few things to do," Ryan offered, his voice displaying an inner humbleness. "It was nothing too complicated."

"Well, whatever it was, it's working now. I wish that I could have that sort of help with the bakery. Matilda here is *gut* at baking, but the business side is not something we do all that well."

Matilda braced herself for what was coming. She knew Ryan would respond. She stared at the peanut butter cake half frosted with the spatula still in the bowl and wondered at the strange turn of events. At one point she had desired that her family get along with and even accept Ryan. Particularly when he had been so determined to attach himself to her hip. Now, she realized, she had let him and that observation alarmed her. How quickly had she let her guard down.

"I can take a look and offer some suggestions," he said. He then wiped the finger that had frosting on it on a dish towel on the counter and tossed it carelessly in Matilda's direction. "We have a slow day at the buggy shop since we've managed to catch up on all the buggies that we needed to fix."

Rebecca glanced at Matilda and smiled before she offered Ryan her best grateful and pleased grin. "That would be *wunderbar*," she said, nodding at the small door next to the shelves of various ingredients they stored there. "My office is in there and —"

The jingle of the front door opening interrupted her. "*Ach*, excuse me Ryan. I will take care of this customer and be right back if you don't mind waiting."

"I surely don't mind waiting," he said, looking at Matilda.

Rebecca disappeared to the front of the bakery. Matilda listened in a surreal haze as her *maemm* chatted happily to an English customer over the various pies they baked. She felt a strong hand cup the back of her arm and then nimble fingers stroked there cautiously as though she was a spooked animal. Those cerulean orbs threatened to melt her into a puddle as her traitorous body leaned toward his touch. Their faces were only centimeters apart with Ryan's head tilted downwards to look at her fully.

"I'm fitting in more. Have you noticed?" he whispered.

The smell of *kaffee* and fresh morning air washed over her face. She felt the tip of her tongue lick her lips and tasted him there. Her lips tingled, and she was captured by a strong desire to close the distance between them.

"I noticed," she breathed back.

Ryan's eyes slipped closed, and he leaned forward to fulfill the one thing that Matilda had been guilty of thinking about all night and morning. Their lips barely brushed before someone cleared their throat loudly before speaking.

"Well, well, well! What do we have going on in here?"

Matilda opened her eyes and saw Lily standing in the doorframe of the back door. Her arms were folded over her chest, and she leaned backwards on her heels as she stared in intense interest. Just like their *maemm*, one of her eyebrows had arched upwards in a rather infuriating fashion that provoked Matilda to step backwards, away from Ryan.

"I can explain this," Matilda said rather weakly.

"*Ach*, please explain yourself out of this one, Matilda." Lily said wryly, shaking her head. "There is no way for you to talk yourself out of this one. No matter what you say, I know what you two were about to do."

Matilda's face burned in embarrassment when Lily shot Ryan a knowing grin. She tried to busy herself with frosting the rest of the cake to avoid the both of them as they grinned at one another. Not only had Ryan won of over her *kinner's* approval, but apparently he had won over her family's approval as well after rescuing her from her buggy accident.

"I knew you two would end up together," Lily announced. "I kept telling *maemm* and *daed* that it was bound to happen sooner or later."

"You told *maemm* and *daed* that?"

"Everyone in the community was guessing when it would happen, Matilda. I've overheard the women coming in here to talk to *maemm* about it, and asking if you two were going to court, eventually."

Ryan's eyes sparkled mischievously, thoroughly enjoying how flustered Matilda was at the news. "Well that explains a few things to me. I still don't know how the whole courtship goes for the older groups."

"I don't think this is suitable conversation to have right now," Matilda said.

"Matilda hasn't explained that to you yet?" Lily asked, ignoring her completely, and entering the kitchen. She frowned mockingly at Matilda. "I thought she would for sure tell you how that all works by now. Especially since there are a few community members that have voiced their hopes in you courting them."

Matilda sought to tamp down a sudden flare of jealousy that fired up from her chest before turning into a smolder. She knew exactly how many women had voiced interest in Ryan since his appearance in the community and his expression of joining the church. It had only increased as the talk turned to his taking the vows with the other new members. Especially those among the women. His opportunity to forge new friendships had greatly increased.

Matilda busied herself by sliding the sheet cake onto a rack but she couldn't rein in her thoughts. While months ago the thought of other women in the community expressing interest in him would have been a relief because it meant she could keep her distance, now it only stoked her jealousy. How to explain this to *Gott*? Many of those women who joined or were ready to join were only a few years older than Lily's age, and inexperienced at being a *fraa*....

Alarmed by her increasing temperamental thoughts, Matilda cleared the counter of the dirty dishes to place them in the soapy water. She finished frosting the cake as Lily and Ryan continued to chat about the buggy business before Rebecca finally appeared from the front.

"I apologize, Ryan. It was old Almina, and she loves to talk up a storm," Rebecca said, laughing lightly. "If you are still available to look over things...."

Ryan pretended to think as he drummed his fingers on the counter before he finally straightened and gave her *maemm* one of his wide, all-encompassing smiles, the one that showed all his teeth. "I sure am, ma'am. Let's take a look, and see whether I can come up with some suggestions." With a quick salute in Lily's direction, Ryan glanced at Matilda briefly, smiled, and followed Rebecca into her office.

The second the door of their *maemm's* office shut Lily was at Matilda's side. She fluttered excitedly next to Matilda, not even realizing that Matilda had just shelved her birthday cake.

"So," Lily asked, unable to keep the excitement out of her voice. "Are you going to tell me about this recent development or will I have to ask Ryan?"

Matilda sighed in irritation, longing for the warm moment that had graced her earlier that morning. It had dissipated into an array of confusing emotions, and she was now in one of those states where she simply wished and prayed for a place to sit in silence so she could think clearly without others looking in. She needed to talk to *Gott* not her sister.

"Please," she said and sighed. "Don't talk to Ryan about it. I'm sure he'd give you an answer that is a bit more exaggerated than the truth."

Lily searched the kitchen for the one chair and pulled it up next to Matilda. "Okay, then tell me your side of it."

"Lily, this is comp —"

"Complicated? What's so complicated about it? Ryan likes you, and I'm pretty sure he's going to ask for courtship after he takes his vows to join the church."

Matilda looked down at her sister, her sixteen year old sister. "It's not that. It's...." She was out of excuses. The once protective walls were crumbling and more than ever, Matilda felt exposed to her conflicted and ever-growing feelings. While one part of her wished that Samuel was still alive so she could talk to him, the other part of her selfishly prayed that in Heaven he wasn't watching. *I've always known...* His words echoed in her mind sadly. "Like I've told you before, it's not easy to let go of a previous marriage or someone that you truly cared about — especially when they were ripped from you."

Lily cocked her head. "You truly cared for Samuel that much?"

"Of course I did," Matilda said, somewhat confused at the question. "He was my *mann*. I cared greatly for him and still do to this day."

Lily placed a gentle hand on Matilda's shoulder. "Please don't take this harshly or the wrong way. *Ja*, you cared for Samuel, but I know that what you feel for Ryan runs much deeper than what feelings you had for Samuel. I don't know how to explain it, but I've seen how you are with them both. You catered to Samuel as a *fraa* would and should, but you acted more comfortably with him. With Ryan, you two are constantly fighting to keep away from each other and even then you both fail. If I can see the difference, I know you can see it too."

Matilda didn't know which surprised her more, Lily's description of the two men or the fact that Lily said it at all. "It-it doesn't matter what I feel. If it's *Gott's* will to keep us apart —"

"Or together," Lily offered.

"— Then, I will follow *Gott's* will despite what I feel in my heart. Even if it breaks my heart again, I will do what *Gott* bids me to do. He has a plan."

"You have such a strong sense of faith, Matilda." Lily said, shaking her head in amazement. "I pray that someday I will have that same amount of faith."

"You will if you just trust *Gott.* I know that it was Samuel's time to join Him in Heaven, and I trust it was for a reason."

"But don't you think that maybe it's because your marriage to Samuel wasn't for the right reasons?"

An imaginary nail dragged itself down the back of Matilda's neck. She reached up with a trembling hand to rub at the prickling skin. *Nee,* it hadn't been for the right reasons, but that had been from her own sinful behavior. Sometimes it was painful to remember that a beautiful blessing from *Gott* came from a night of temptation. She sought to ease the tension. "No one truly knows what *Gott's* will is, Lily. I wish that I knew, but if I knew then I wouldn't have much faith in Him. Why is this such a concern to you anyway?"

"You're my sister. I only want to see you happy, and I don't truly think you've been happy for a while."

Matilda's eyes blurred with tears, but before she could voice her appreciation, Ryan emerged from their *maemm's* office with a few sheets of paper in hand. Their eyes meet instantly, and he motioned to hers with an inquisitive frown. She hastily palmed her eyes dry. Rebecca looked down at papers happily when he handed them over to her. "*Danka* for all your suggestions. I will definitely put these lists to *gut* use," she said, and then immediately handed them over to Matilda and Lily. "Aren't these *wunderbar?* Ryan has helped me organize our inventory of ingredients so it's cheaper and easier for us to keep track of what we have and don't."

"*Wunderbar,*" Matilda said, glancing down at the spreadsheets. She gently placed them on the counter so that the flour or anything else wouldn't get onto the paper. "I will take a look at them once I am finished with this cake."

"You're not finished with the cake?" Rebecca's gaze floated to the still half-frosted cake, and a frown filled her face. "I thought you would've finished this before Lily returned. The surprise is ruined."

"It's fine, *maemm,*" Lily said, smiling at Matilda. "It's not even a surprise since we do this *every* birthday."

"It's also my fault. I distracted Matilda for a few minutes as well when she was trying to frost the cake," Ryan added.

Overwhelmed by the sudden acceptance of Ryan, her own confused feelings, and the last few weeks, Matilda faced Rebecca. "Do you think that I could possibly have a moment to cool down?" Matilda asked tightly, handing a spatula to Lily. "I am feeling a bit light headed, and I think I need some time to pray."

Rebecca looked at her in puzzlement. "Pray?" She echoed. "What are you in need of prayer for? Maybe we could do it together."

Matilda fought back the frustration and maintained a forced smile. "For some strength. I'm feeling a bit weak."

Awash with worry, her mother came to the rescue. "If you're feeling sick then you should go home to rest for a few hours. I don't want you wearing yourself out on your sister's birthday. I can pick your *kinner* up from the schoolhouse."

"*Danka*," Matilda answered with relief.

She washed her hands quickly before starting in the direction of the door. Her hand barely touched the brass knob when Ryan's voice stopped her, "Do you need a ride, Mattie? I can give you one if you are feeling sick."

She winced at the nickname. Not only did her *kinner* hear it but now her *maemm*? Matilda peeked over her shoulder to see the wheels in her *maemm's* brain beginning to turn and hurriedly opened the door.

"*Nee*. I'll be fine," she said and fled. She practically leaped out of the stuffy kitchen, slamming the door shut before anyone else could say a word, and ran as fast as she could away.

CHAPTER NINE

S aturday morning was the first Farmers Market to start off the spring season. The town was abuzz with tourists despite the dreary clouds looming overhead, threatening to downpour without notice. Matilda arranged the pies on the cooling racks to attract attention and then sliced a few pieces of apple pie as samplers for anyone who wished to try a piece before purchasing a pie. She also set out a platter of whoopie pies as well, knowing that they would be gone shortly from how popular they were.

"It's a shame that this weather isn't cooperating," Rebecca said. She placed little plastic forks with the slices of pie and looked up at the dark clouds. "I pray that it doesn't start to rain. It would be a very cold rain from how the air feels this morning."

Matilda scanned the crowd of Englischers for any sight of her *kinner*. Her sons had long since disappeared to play with their friends, but Rosella, too, had slipped off to avoid helping at the stand. While her oldest knew how to bake and cook, it was never something that she particularly seemed fond of doing and only helped when needed.

"I pray that it doesn't rain too," Matilda said, and finally spotted Rosella talking with Betty a few feet away. "If it does, I will take Matthew home. I don't wish for him to fall ill again from the cold."

"And you too, Matilda," Rebecca added sternly. "I don't want you to fall ill either. I can handle the stand alone if it starts to rain."

"Are you sure? I know that Lily left last night..." She trailed off at the concerned grimace contorting Rebecca's tired face. Friday night, the first weekend of her Rumspringa, Lily left their tight knit community to spend the weekend in Denver with a group of friends. Obviously, the two of them shared the same concern over Lily's wellbeing. Had Rebecca felt this concerned when Matilda left for her own Rumspringa? She dimly remembered Rebecca encouraging her to go and sow her wild oats before committing herself to *Gott,* but there hadn't been any real concern expressed. "How are you feeling about Lily leaving?"

Rebecca smiled wearily. "Her faith is in *Gott's* hands. I only pray that she doesn't get into trouble while she is away."

"Were you ever worried for me?"

"*Nee.*" Rebecca said, shaking her head. "I always knew how confident you were within yourself and faith in *Gott.* You didn't even want to leave at first. I never worried about you giving in to temptation."

A sharp pain erupted in the center of Matilda's chest. She looked away to hide the tears flooding her eyes at her *maemm's* unperturbed opinion of her faith. How could her family be so confident in her faith? Shame flooded her at their confidence in her faith. If they knew the truth of what had actually happened on Rumspringa, the reason behind her rushed marriage to Samuel, and the truth behind Rosella's conception, they would be ashamed and even upset at her for keeping it a secret. She had given in to the temptation, and losing Samuel years afterwards had felt like punishment enough. Now, the object of her temptation stood on the other side of the Farmers Market.

A light rain drizzled down upon them for the next few hours. Matilda stood beneath the white tent with Rebecca, talking to Englischers that came to their stand, and giving baking advice whenever asked.

"*Ja*, Granny apples are the best for pies. *Nee*, use more flour with the high altitude to keep the crust fluffy," she would say over and over again with that polite smile of hers.

When the last of the whoopee pies were gone, Matilda left the dry confines of the tent to find Rosella helping Betty fold a quilt to put into an Englischer's bag to keep it shielded from the rain.

"We need your help over at the baking stand," Matilda said, smiling politely at Betty who looked disappointed in losing someone other than her siblings to talk to.

Rosella nodded. She handed the folded blanket to Betty before slipping into a rain jacket, flipping the hood up to keep herself dry as possible as the two of them ducked out from beneath the tent. "There is another batch of whoopie pies at the bakery," Matilda told her as they walked along the wet grass. "If you take Pepper and the buggy, you won't get rained on as much while bringing them here."

"*Ja*, I'll be back shortly then." Rosella ducked her head further as the rain splattered upon their shoulders a bit harder. She hurried out to where the buggy was currently parked and to the field where Pepper was grazing happily despite the rain.

"Did I hear something about whoopie pies?"

Matilda turned around to look at Ryan from underneath the hood of her own rain jacket. Rain drops dripped from the rim of his straw hat and onto his broad shoulders, trailing down the curves of his arms. He, too, wore a plain gray rain jacket that was buttoned up tightly, but the bottom cuffs of his trousers were soaked from the wet grass. None of the wetness or the cold seemed to bother him from the way his eyes sparkled. Before she could even summon up a reason to distance herself or find an excuse to leave, she felt herself melting when he smiled at her.

"*Ja*, we've sold out of them. I baked a few batches this morning in case we ran out."

"You baked this morning?" Ryan echoed, clearly amazed at the time she'd already spent for the Farmers Market.

"A while, but I don't mind."

"Does your *haus* need repairs? I could always fix them or even give you money if you need it."

She smiled, touched by his concern, and said, "The extra money will help out the community with repairs that need be done or if someone is in need of it."

"So all the proceeds go to the church, is that right?" Ryan asked.

"If we don't have any immediate need for the money. I'm trying to sell as many pies as I can to pay the community back for Samuel's hospital bills...." She stopped at that. The bills for the longest time never seemed to end, even when the community generously came forward to help pay the debt off. They pitched in without asking and even helped set up payment plans for it to be paid off within a few short months. Despite how broken and shattered her heart had felt then, the small pieces that remained were touched by her community's generosity. It was a bitter and cruel reminder that Samuel was gone despite everyone's best efforts.

Ryan smiled gently. "I know how that feels. I used to get bills all the time from all the various medical centers I took mom to. Half the time I felt like calling to tell them that they would be paid in time, but to give me a few months to accept that she was gone. Unfortunately money makes the world go around."

"Only in some areas," Matilda said, and then smiled at him, remembering Ryan's participation. "How are the Englischers enjoying the buggy rides?"

"They seem pretty happy about it. The kids are more interested in it, but the rain makes it hard to not be miserable. I've been thinking, maybe I should breed swans and have a pond where people can pay to feed them bits of bread."

"Now that would be an idea no Amish community had ever heard of," Matilda said, laughing at the thought.

"Exactly. Maybe someday I could do that." He grinned widely, once again showing off all his white teeth. Over his shoulder, Matilda caught sight of a group of young English *kinner* climbing into one of the buggies. "Looks like you have another group of *kinner* wishing to ride a buggy," she said, pointing to them.

"Looks like it. I'll be back then, and you better save me at least one whoopie pie," he threatened, but winked playfully before heading to the group of children.

Matilda chuckled to herself as she returned to the baking stand to help Rebecca slice another pie to hand out as a sample. She looked up when she felt a presence in front of the stand, and immediately reeled back in shock to see who it was.

Olivia stood beneath the tent. She was dressed in what looked like a pair of tight jeans, knee-high leather boots, and an expensive rain coat. Her blonde hair, the same color as Ryan's and Rosella's, was twisted up into a messy and frizzy bun from the rain. A red tinge circled her crystalline blue eyes, and her red lips were pressed into a thin line, suggesting her discomfort of being here.

"Olivia?" Matilda managed to say as politely as possible. She had never enjoyed Olivia's rather forward personality, but she remained friendly through *Gott's* presence. "I didn't expect you. Ryan never mentioned you would be here."

"That's because Ryan doesn't know I'm here," Olivia said curtly. She glanced over her shoulder, undoubtedly looking for him. "Do you know where he is? The last letter he wrote me said that you and he were starting to pick up a relationship again, so I assume you know of his whereabouts."

Matilda tensed. While that statement wasn't exactly untrue, she didn't wish for it to be announced by an Englischer in front of her *maemm*. "He just left to give some children a ride in a buggy. He should be —"

"Would you deliver a message to him?" Olivia asked, cutting over her. "I have to make a phone call back at the hotel."

Annoyed by the bossy attitude, Matilda forced herself to nod and asked *Gott* for more strength. She would do anything at this point to make sure Olivia didn't rattle of anything else.

"I didn't want to say this to someone else without telling him first," Olivia said, sighing heavily. "But tell him it's about his ex-wife, Amy."

The world slowed down around Matilda as she stared at Olivia in complete and utter shock. Ex-wife? The phrase repeated itself dubiously over and over inside of her mind. Ryan would have surely told her something like that. "I'm sorry. Did you say ex-wife?"

Olivia gave her a quick glance and frowned. "Yes," she said slowly, "I did say ex-wife. Ryan and Amy were married for a few years before they divorced. He didn't tell you any of this?"

"No… He… No, never."

Matilda was genuinely at loss for words. Flipping through the past year's worth of conversations, she desperately tried to remember any mention of an ex-wife. When none came to mind, it became painfully clear that Ryan had chosen to keep his previous marriage a secret from her in particular. Matilda glanced over at Rebecca who, too, seemed quite surprised by the revelation and watched as the trust that had been gained over time dissipated into suspicion again.

Tears stung her eyes unexpectedly at the hurt building up within her. Why would he have decided to keep such a thing quiet? *Gott* would have surely spoken to him through their ways of living to remain humble and honest about the past. And yet, he didn't tell her.

Matilda's face burned when Olivia shot her a strange look.

"He never told you about Amy?"

Matilda looked away. "Obviously not."

"I told you, Matilda." Rebecca said softly, and laid a hand on Matilda's shoulder when she jumped in surprise. "I knew there was something that he wasn't being honest about."

Olivia eyed Rebecca. Her face, usually so placid and calm, rippled with suspicion. "Does it matter to the Amish if someone were married before joining? Or is this going to mess up his plans on being here forever? Not that I'm all that hung up on his joining your community but it is something he wants."

"No," Matilda answered, sensing a confrontation brewing. "It doesn't matter to us. We're just surprised is all since he had never mentioned anything."

If Olivia didn't believe it, she chose not to make another comment. Instead, she smoothed a manicured hand over her frizzy hair and looked around the Farmers Market once more. "Well, I don't know why he didn't tell you. Sometimes my brother keeps things a secret for no reason besides not wanting to talk about them. So, knowing how he is, I guess I'll have to tell you first."

"Maybe you should wait —"

"He won't respond if I don't tell you the reason why I'm here. I know how my brother is, and what his relationship with Amy was like," Olivia said dryly. Before Matilda could ask what it was like out of pure curiosity, Olivia continued. "Tell him that Amy died in a car crash last week, and that her family would really appreciate it if he could come to the funeral. They might have been only married for a few years, but she still meant a lot to our family…."

Tears glistened in Olivia's eyes. She quickly turned away to hide them, wiping them away with the pads of her fingers.

Matilda felt a bit of surprise at Olivia's open expression of grief, and she briefly closed her eyes to pray to *Gott* for the grace not to be jealous over Olivia's obvious approval of Ryan's marriage to Amy. She knew it was not a proper time to feel such emotions, if ever. She also prayed for Amy and how heartbroken her family must feel. Matilda remembered Samuel's family, and how devastated they had been when he passed away. They had traveled all the way from Lancaster, his whole family, to gather at the gravesite and to help Matilda with chores around the *haus*. *Gott* had been working in her life without her even knowing it. Yet even with the influx of constant voices, the *haus* had still felt empty without Samuel in it. Despite knowing that Samuel was now with *Gott*, it never dulled the constant ache of wishing for his presence to return to their lives.

"I'm sorry to hear that she has passed. I pray for her and her family," Matilda said, her heart open with compassion. "And for you too. I can see you that you were close to her."

"As will our community pray," Rebecca added.

Olivia nodded at them both before looking to Matilda again. For once, those often crystalline orbs showed a touch of vulnerability, a sight Matilda sympathized with greatly. Olivia adjusted the strap of her purse and bid them goodbye before disappearing into the gray mist that enveloped the market. The second Olivia was out of earshot, Matilda let out a strangled breath and turned to look at Rebecca in shock.

"I didn't imagine that, did I?"

"*Nee,* you didn't imagine any of it," Rebecca said, shaking her head with a disappointed sigh. "As I said, I had a feeling that there was something that Ryan wasn't being honest about."

"After everything we talked about I —"

Once again a burst of tears appeared. There was no mistaking the sting of hurt that burned at the center of her chest. Why? The question kept echoing inside of her mind. Why hadn't he told her?

The cold rain continued to come down a bit harder. Raindrops pattered loudly on the white tent above their heads and dripped off the edges of the tent. A boom of thunder in the distance promised an approaching storm and heavier rain. Matilda wrapped her arms tightly around herself to fight of the cold that had seeped painfully into her bones.

"Go home, Matilda," her *maemm* said softly, placing a hand on Matilda's trembling shoulder. "Your *daed* will be here shortly to help pick up, and I can take the *kinner* for a while."

Through the rain and crowds of Englischers, a buggy reappeared with children gleefully jumping into Ryan's arms as he helped them off. The sight of his grin made her stomach churn in denial. Impulsively, she wished to do what her *maemm* suggested, to leave. But she couldn't, she had promised to deliver Olivia's message to Ryan, and no amount of anger or hurt would make her feel justified in keeping such information from him.

"I have to tell Ryan," Matilda said.

"Matilda —"

"It's the right thing to do, *maemm,* and you know that it is. What would *Gott* think if I didn't say anything?"

Rebecca sighed in defeat. "You're right. Go on. If you need to leave afterward, I will understand."

Matilda flipped up the hood of her jacket and ducked out from beneath the tent. The rain started to come down harder in a sheet of gray, but she could barely hear the sound of drops splattering on the hood of her jacket over the thumping of her heart. She jogged on trembling knees, nearly slipping a few times on the slick grass before finally making it to Ryan's side as a little girl jumped into his arms to run away quickly to take shelter against the rain. Thunder cracked above them followed by quick flashes of lightening as streams of bodies darted beneath the tents for protection until the storm passed.

"Mattie?" Ryan shouted over the boom of thunder head hunched against the onslaught. "What's wrong?"

"I have to tell you something important," she shouted back.

The cold rain slapped her forehead as Ryan grabbed her by the elbow and hauled her effortlessly up into the buggy. She shivered violently as she sat on the seat, while Ryan darted around the buggy to climb into the driver's side. Her prayer *kapp* was soaked, as was the collar of her dress, from the rain slipping down the back of her neck.

"This storm is crazy. Do you think they'll cancel the rest of the Farmers Market?" Ryan asked, his eyes focused on the sky above them.

Matilda didn't answer. She was too busy trying to figure out how she could she tell him Olivia's news without demanding answers. There had been only one time in her life when she ever had to deliver news of death and that had been to Samuel's parents in Lancaster. Bishop Abraham had suggested using the bakery's phone to call Samuel's *maemm* at her own bakery, but how hard it was then to think of the right and comforting words. There never was comforting words at first.

So, she blurted out, "Your sister was here, and she needs to talk to you."

Ryan looked away from the sky to Matilda in surprise. Rain drops trailed down his forehead and a few nestled in the arch of his eyebrow. "My sister was here? What did she say? Is everything okay?"

"*Nee*, I mean," she backtracked at the fear filling his eyes. "Your sister is fine. It's about Amy...your ex-wife."

For a moment, Matilda feared that Ryan hadn't heard her. His cerulean eyes stared unblinkingly at her completely devoid of any emotion. She swallowed down the bulge inside her throat, waiting for him to speak first. For the longest moment, he didn't move or talk.

Finally, he stirred to ask, "What about my ex-wife?"

His cool tone sent chills down her spine. All the questions that were circling inside her mind were going to go unanswered judging from how Ryan's eyes were narrowed in suspicion and aloofness.

"Your sister said that she wants to tell you in person. She's at the hotel here in town." It wasn't exactly a lie. Whatever apparently had happened between Ryan and Amy didn't end well, and she didn't want to be the person to deliver the message.

"Don't lie to me. My sister knows me well enough that I am not going to go talk to her without knowing what this is about. So, what is it?"

Matilda chewed on her bottom lip until she tasted the tang of blood. The words were a jumbled mess as they slipped from the tip of her tongue in resignation. "Your sister told me that your ex-wife died in a car accident. She wanted to tell you in person, but...."

The first glimmer of emotion filled Ryan's eyes as he abruptly looked away to hide the grief, sucking in a harsh breath. He gazed unseeingly out the buggy window, and was clearly oblivious to the rain splattering against the buggy roof and thunder booming above them.

"I'm sorry," was all she could think of to say.

Ryan gave a sharp nod to her words. Unsure of what to do, Matilda reached out a tentative hand to rest it on his shoulder. He immediately flinched out from beneath the touch, shaking his head. Her hand fell uselessly to the seat between them as hurt tears stung her eyes.

Grief, she reminded herself, wasn't an easy emotion to deal with. No matter how strong a person appeared to be, it could still knock them down.

"Don't," he said quietly, and turned away to close his eyes in what appeared to be prayer from how his lips moved silently.

Despite her own raging river of emotions, Matilda forced herself to sit still. The godly thing to do would be to offer comfort in a time of grief, but it was incredibly hard given the questions that threatened to spew from her lips. She prayed for strength and guidance on how to handle this situation, but found herself swirling with a tumult of surprise.

She bit the tip of her tongue in a vain effort to keep quiet, but the question tumbled out into the cold buggy air, "Why didn't you say anything about being married before?"

Ryan scoffed out a laugh. He turned his head to gaze at her, smiling darkly. "I was wondering how long it would take you to ask that. You were fidgeting."

"Can you blame me?"

"*Nee*, I can't blame you." He said, and shrugged his shoulders. "What do you want me to say, Mattie? Assure you that the marriage didn't work and that she was an awful person?"

"I obviously know that it didn't work out. I —why didn't you say anything? After everything I told you —"

"I didn't tell you because I didn't want you to think of me the way I used to be. *I* didn't want to think of the way I used to be," Ryan interrupted. The emotion that had glimmered in Ryan's eyes was now visible. Guilt darkened his expression, and it had her heart sinking. "I wanted to put the past in the past and give myself to *Gott*. Amy and I got married way too young. She worked as my receptionist, and I imagine you can fill in the rest."

Matilda didn't want to fill in the rest. It was irrational to feel jealous over a previous marriage when she had been married previously too. They both had their previous lives and relationships. Of course, there was one big difference. His wife, ex-wife, *had* been alive. She forced herself to remain calm. "What happened?"

Ryan drummed his fingers on his thighs. "We married out of lust and fell out of it. It was a mutual thing to both move on. It wasn't huge falling out... I... we stayed pretty good friends for a while."

"Why did you keep this a secret?" Matilda asked, the question burning inside of her head. With every second that ticked by and every clap of thunder, the hurt and anger began to make its way up her throat. "After everything that we talked about —"

"I cheated on her, Mattie! That's why I didn't want to say it, and why I didn't want to talk about it. I've avoided Amy and her family for the past few years because I couldn't look at them without feeling like scum. That's why. Okay?" At her stunned silence, Ryan continued on in a low voice, "And don't act like you don't have your own secrets that you're keeping from me. You're hiding something, too. I know it. You know it."

Matilda looked away in part from his blazing eyes to hide her own guilty expression, but mostly because of the shock that rocked her. She felt cornered. What secret did he suspect? He had her in a corner and knew it.

"That's what I thought," he said. "You wanted me to tell you the truth and I did. What are *you* hiding?"

She bit down, harder, on the tip of her tongue. Every inch of her quivered in an effort to stay contained. "It's complicated," she started.

"It always is when it comes to you, Mattie," Ryan said, shaking his head at her. His lips thinned into a straight line. "I have to leave and find my sister. If you can excuse me...."

Tears blurred her vision and she remained rooted to the seat. She heard Ryan let out an impatient breath as his arm brushed against her stomach to open the buggy door.

"I have to go," he said, in a voice as cold as the rain splattering around them. "I have to go to the funeral and see her family. We can talk when I come back."

Maybe it was the cold or how wrong their conversation had gone, but the idea of Ryan leaving their community to attend his ex-wife's funeral didn't sit well with her. They had progressed greatly with their friendship that bordered on more, and both of them had discovered a stronger sense of faith within one another. She felt torn by these revelations. Yet, irrational as it was, she was afraid that Ryan would be swayed by his old world and not want to return to the community and to her.

"If you even want to come back," she choked out through her tears.

Afraid to give him time to retaliate, she slipped out into the rainy morning. Her heart raced so fast now that it left her feeling dizzy. Still, a small hopeful part of her waited for Ryan to open the door and call her back but there was nothing but silence.

She glanced over her shoulder as the buggy started forward. Horse hooves sloshed through the wet grass, and she took a hasty step backwards to avoid her toes being run over by the wheels. Rain drops intermingled with the saltiness of her tears as she watched him leave, knowing all the while that there was a definite possibility that he would not return.

CHAPTER TEN

He has an ex-wife?"

The question hung in the air as Lily stood next to Matilda by the stove and absently stirred a pot of boiling green beans with butter. After Lily's return to the community on Sunday for church after another Rumspringa excursion, Matilda for the first time sought out her sister's ears. She was on the brink of exploding from the new information and from the hurt of what had happened at the Farmers Market two weeks ago. Lily agreed to help Matilda with dinner on Monday night so they could talk without others listening in on their conversation.

"*Ja*, well, he did. I pray for her family since I found out," Matilda said. She grabbed a can of seasonings from the shelf above the stove and shook it with more force than necessary over the freshly plucked chicken. "I just don't understand it. After everything that he and I talked about, why wouldn't he say something about an ex-wife?"

"Maybe he didn't think it was important? Englischer's look at marriage differently than we Amish."

"They do, but it's not that. He was devastated when I told him. She had been a huge part of his life then at some point. Like Samuel was to me, so I just don't understand why he hadn't told anyone."

"Maybe he told the Bishop and asked for him to keep it quiet?"

Matilda paused at that. It was possible he did mention it to the church but had decided not tell her for the reason he had stated in the buggy. Yet, she had her doubts. Clearly, Ryan didn't understand that having an ex-wife in the outside world did not mean the same thing to the Amish.

"How did you find out about all this exactly?" Lily asked.

Matilda set the seasonings back on the shelf. She rubbed down any clumps on the freshly plucked skin before cleaning her hands and setting the chicken in the oven to bake for the next hour or so. The patter of rain filled the warm *haus*. "Ryan's sister came to the Farmers Market on Saturday to look for him. She thought we were — well, that part doesn't matter, but I had to pass the message along."

"Crazy," Lily said and whistled, all the while shaking her head in amazement. "I leave for a short time for rumpringa and something like that happens. What are the odds? It's usually so very quiet here."

"I'm still reeling from it myself. I pray all the time to understand what his motives were to keep that quiet." And pray for guidance on forgiving him from keeping a secret when she kept one herself.

Lily kept up her barrage of questions. "You've never had a secret once before in your life?"

Matilda's thoughts soared to Rosella, who would be back within an hour or two from helping her *maemm* at the bakery. Watching Ryan leave the Farmers Market without even sparing her a goodbye, tears streaming from the corners of his eyes for a woman he had at one time clearly loved, left doubt residing once more in Matilda's heart. What other things had he not told her? Scenarios flicked through her mind in rapid succession, things she hadn't even wished to think about. Would he come back after the funeral? It had been weeks now with no word from him.

Those questions and more had swirled violently within her mind throughout church the Sunday after Ryan left as the community prayed for the woman's family after the Bishop had delivered the news. She had watched then as her community bowed their heads in prayer. Seeking *Gott's* council had been the only thing that eased the trouble within her, and it also dulled the ache of being hurt. How could she be upset over him keeping a secret when she kept one too?

A secret capable of destroying and crushing everything within its path.

"I suppose you're right. We all have secrets," Matilda said eventually. "I don't know why this is bothering me so much."

"Because you care for him, and he cares for you." Lily held up a hand when Matilda opened her mouth, "Argue it all you want, *shvista*. I know there's some sort of relationship developing between the two of you again. The whole community can see it, but you seem to be the only one trying to deny it. Mattie —"

She ignored the obvious remark on her nickname. "It's just not that easy to let go of Samuel, or to accept someone who may not even stay here. I told you before. Now he's left, Lily, to go back to the Englischers and their world."

"To attend a funeral," Lily corrected. "You're letting your imagination and doubt run away from you. The church understands that not everyone is willing or able to follow our faith, but that doesn't make them any less of a person. They deserve *Gott's* love as much as we do."

Matilda wordlessly held out a glass casserole dish for Lily to fill with the buttered beans. She watched with a small smile as her sister's nimble fingers sprinkled shredded cheese over the steaming greens.

"When have you gained so much wisdom?" she asked teasingly, but relieved to hear those words coming from Lily's mouth. While the revelation about Ryan's ex-wife had plagued her, so did her concern for Lily while dealing with the Englischer wordily lifestyle. It seemed that Lily had returned with a stronger sense of faith.

"A majority of it I learned through church and from all of you," Lily said. "Maybe, too, a bit of personal experience this past weekend."

"Well, let's have some tea, and you can tell me about it. I don't want to think about Ryan anymore."

Once they finished wiping the counters clean, they steeped two mugs of peppermint tea, and sat in the living room in front of the wood stove. Lily perched herself delicately on the edge of the couch cushion, holding back a plain white curtain to peer outside. "I have never seen it rain like this before during the spring nor remember it being this cold. I pray that it lifts soon. I am getting tired of wearing rain boots all the time."

Lily stretched out her foot to reveal a battered rain boot. Mud and water stains coated every inch of the slick texture. They laughed while taking a sip of the hot tea dosed with a spoonful of honey. The warm liquid coated Matilda's throat soothingly as she stared out the window at the gray clouds.

"At least we won't be in a drought this year if the rain keeps up. The only real danger is if it continues to be cold into April."

"That's true, I guess. When it rained in Denver, the smell was... funny." Lily said. She looked at Matilda in confusion when she snorted out a laugh, "What? It smelt weird there, and there was a constant orange haze in the sky. Do you remember that?"

"It's been a few years since I've been there, Lily. I have a feeling that things might have changed since then."

"You're right on that. I've never seen so many buildings or cars or Englischers all in one place. *Ach*, and that noise. I could hardly sleep."

Matilda nodded in understanding. "*Ja*, I remember not being able to sleep. I bet coming back to the community felt *wunderbar.*"

"It did, but I was also kind of sad when I left, too. At the same time, I felt relieved to be away from the constant noise. I don't know how some decide to leave the quiet and peace here. I wouldn't be able to handle the noise."

"And what did you all do while you were there?" Matilda asked, leaning back in her rocking chair.

Lily stirred the contents of her tea with her pointer finger. When she looked back up, a red hue burned brightly in the center of her cheeks. "Just the same thing that everyone else did. We drank a couple of beers and dressed in English clothes and went to some stupid party. You know, a party with a whole bunch of drunk people and loud music. It really wasn't what I thought it would be." As an afterthought, she added pleadingly, "Please don't tell *maemm* or *daed* any of that."

"It'll stay between us."

They shared a smile before Lily continued on in a soft voice, "I know that the church encourages us to wait until our eighteenth birthday to make sure, but I don't want to wait that long."

"They only advise that you wait so that you feel the decision is right. It's a big commitment to make."

"But you joined the church right after your Rumspringa."

Matilda dropped her eyes to hide the flash of pain. It was on the tip of her tongue, to finally tell someone her secret and the reason behind her hastily arranged baptism and marriage, but a horse whinnying in the distance stopped her from forming a coherent sentence. She set her cup of tea down on the little end table next to her, equally relieved but disappointed at the interruption. She forced herself to swallow the secret once again and felt the weight of it settle into her center.

How much longer could she hold this in? Every day that passed with it nestled deeply within her, the heavier it grew.

"Who's here?" Lily asked. She, too, set her tea down and twisted around on the couch to look outside. "I see a buggy, but I don't see Rosella or Matthew and Isaac."

"It's probably them. *Maemm* insisted that I rest today, and she would bring my *kinner* home."

"Um, it's not *maemm*."

The surprise in Lily's voice froze Matilda in the rocking chair, her hands braced on the arm rests to stand up. Her heart beat painfully when Lily turned to look at Matilda.

"You'll never guess who is walking up to the *haus*."

Matilda clutched the rocking chair. "Who?"

"Ryan."

The sunlight felt *wunderbar* on the sensitive skin of Matilda's face. She tilted her head upwards to gaze at the clear sky, rejoicing that this particular Sunday morning would remain a warm one. Two months had passed since the cold weather of March and April, bringing a warm front of air that promised summer. The smell of brown sugar filled her tidy kitchen as the morning light danced along the floorboards. A shoofly pie baked happily inside the oven as Matilda moved about the kitchen to prepare other meals for church.

Footsteps down the hallway followed by Rosella's voice washed over Matilda as she turned to watch her daughter enter the kitchen. Her honey-blonde hair was freshly clean and smoothed back in a perfect bun while she smoothed out any wrinkles in her purple dress.

"Morning, Ma. Do you need any help?"

"*Gut* morning. *Ja*, there is a shoofly pie in the oven that needs to come out."

Rosella nodded as she slipped on oven mitts to grab the hot pie from the oven. She placed it carefully on a cooling rack and smiled. "Are you excited about today?"

Today, church would be different. After weeks of preparing for baptism, there would be new members within their community taking the vow and joining their church. A shiver of anticipation went through Matilda thinking about Ryan finally completing his testing period and his preparations to join over the last few weeks. While a year ago the thought would have made her sick with nerves, it filled her with joy to know that Ryan was truly devoting himself to *Gott*. The trials of the past year had not swayed him from his path to join.

The past was the past, she reminded herself daily, whenever a thought of Samuel popped into her mind or a question about Ryan's past.

"*Ja*," she said, smiling at Rosella, "Just think. It will be you taking the vow soon."

"It seems so far away…." Rosella sighed longingly.

Matilda smoothed a hand over Rosella's arm, trying to hold back the tears that wanted to surface when she thought of what would also happen sooner than later. Rosella's Rumspringa was approaching fast, and soon it would be her daughter going to experience the Englischer world. The thought filled her with sadness, fear, and even a bit of excitement to know that Rosella was growing up to be a beautiful young woman.

"It'll be here before you know it. Are your *bruders* up?"

"*Ja*, last I checked they were bathing."

They finished cleaning the kitchen right as Matthew and Isaac bounded down the stairs. With each of her *kinner* holding a bowl or plate of food, they managed to leave the *haus* in a timely manner that would get them to the Byler's barn before church services started. The traces of the cold front that had clung to the valley stubbornly for the past few weeks had finally given away to the promise of a hot summer; something that filled Matilda with thanks. Next Saturday they would plant seeds in the garden for the fall now that the weather had returned to its normal dry heat.

There was an excited buzz in the Byler barn when they arrived. Matilda helped push the benches into neatly aligned rows while keeping an eye out for Ryan to appear from a tack room where he was being questioned by Bishop Abraham. She remembered the day she took her kneeling vow, and being thoroughly questioned on her understanding of what it meant to devote herself to *Gott* and adhere to the *Ordnung*. Her knees had trembled with nerves, but it was worth it to see Samuel smiling proudly at her.

While their minister started with their usual hymnal songs, Matilda allowed her eyes to drift closed as she prayed for continued guidance. Now that Ryan was joining the church, she had little idea of what would happen to their relationship. Their feelings for one another had remained unspoken since Ryan's return to the community. Instead of talk, he had focused on his resolve to join the church. She had no idea if he wished to pursue a courtship.

The tack door slipped open as the minister finished their hymns. Matilda sat up a bit straighter as Bishop Abraham walked out with Ryan behind him. She watched as those cerulean blues scanned the crowd of *kapps* to land on Matilda's. The corner of Ryan's lips curved up into a wide smile when their eyes connected. She bit the inside of her lips to contain the giddy smile that wanted to spread across her own face.

Joy filled Matilda as she leaned forward to watch as Bishop Abraham motioned for Ryan to kneel down on the floor in front of the congregation. The minister slowly poured water through the Bishop's hands and to drip down onto Ryan's forehead, wet trails caressing his tanned forehead. When he opened his eyes, an expression of reverence filled them.

It was official; he was now a part of their church, a part of their community, and now a part of Matilda's life. He had finally taken the last strides that would allow him to live his life with *Gott* and commit to follow their customs and ways, as she did.

Matilda could barely contain her excitement as church finally concluded. Standing up from the bench, she made to head in Ryan's direction when a hand cupped her elbow. Her *maemm's* eyes were full of caution and disapproval. She still had yet to forgive Ryan for not telling Matilda about his previous marriage but would in time, Matilda prayed.

"Please be careful, Matilda."

Matilda smiled assuringly at Rebecca. "The past is the past, *maemm*. He wasn't the only one with secrets."

"You have secrets?"

Matilda was thankfully spared an answer when Ryan appeared in front of them. Drops of water trailed down the side of his temples as he placed his black hat back on top of his fair head.

"I never thought that would feel the way it did," he said, his eyes filled with a new light.

"*Ach*? How did it feel?" Matilda asked.

Ryan pursed his lips in thought for a moment. "Bittersweet," he said, and then smiled, "but it was the right choice. I know in my heart that devoting myself to *Gott* and church is the right thing for me to do right now."

"Right now?" Rebecca piped up curiously. "Devoting your life to *Gott* and the *Ordnung* is a lifetime commitment."

Matilda's eyes drifted closed at her *maemm's* stern words. Doubt started to bubble beneath her skin as well but was quickly soothed when Ryan spoke. "*Ja*, it is, and I'm well aware of it. I don't commit myself to anything if I don't feel comfortable enough to honor that commitment."

Other members of their community came to Ryan's side and congratulated him with handshakes and friendly embraces. Matilda managed to slip away from her *maemm* to make sure her *kinner* had plates of food before Ryan motioned for her to follow him out to the field alongside the barn. The smell of hay and dry summer air filled Matilda's nose pleasantly as she hitched up the blue skirts of her dress to walk more easily through the field. Blades of dry grass tickled at her calves and ankles. They stopped out of earshot but remained in plain sight.

A nervous tension crackled through the air between them. Ryan fidgeted with his hands, and at one point he reached down to pick absently at some blades of grass. She watched him nervously as well, twisting her hands into fists and then unclenching them.

"I wanted to talk to you away from everyone else," he said eventually and raised his eyes to look at her. "We haven't had a chance to talk over the past couple of weeks since I returned."

"You've been busy with preparing for this day. I completely understand."

"I have been, but I still owe you an explanation over why I haven't told you about Amy. I simply wanted to let go of a painful part of my past and only look to the future."

Matilda placed a hand on his shoulder. "I have prayed about it for weeks, and it occurred to me the other day that it shouldn't matter anymore. The past is our past, but that doesn't stop us from having a future…." *Together.* She swallowed the word before it slipped out. She had no idea where Ryan's heart resided or whether he wished to be with her. She knew there were still parts of him that she didn't know but hoped that that those discoveries would still occur.

"Always so positive, Mattie, and forgiving too," he said, a warm fondness touching his eyes. "I wanted to tell you that I didn't just join to be a part of the Amish way because I felt like it was the right thing, but I also wanted to be with you, too. *Gott* has brought us together. I can feel Him working in our lives like you always said. It's been one of the biggest reasons why I have stayed here."

Her heart pounded at the soft spoke confession. Never before had someone admitted such a thing to her. While she had grown to love Samuel over time, it was a mutual understanding that he married her to protect her from the negative backlash of her sinful behavior. Their love for one another had never felt like what Matilda felt in the present with fire sizzling through her veins, and finally after much prayer, she accepted it.

"I'm glad you came back after you left," she told him, smiling shyly. "I was worried you wouldn't come back after being away from here."

Long nimble fingers threaded through her own. Matilda shivered in pleasure at the feeling of Ryan's hand in her own and didn't bother to pull away. His hand squeezed hers comfortingly.

"The whole time I was away I wanted to be back. I'm sorry for how I acted that day."

"I'm sorry for how I acted, too."

The sunlight bore down on them hotly. The tips of Ryan's bangs were still damp from the water when she tentatively reached up to brush her fingers across his forehead.

"I want to be with you and only you," he whispered, eyes closed in apparent pleasure at her touch. "How do we go on from here?"

"Well, there's courtship," she whispered back, and nearly jolted out her skin when Ryan's hands suddenly rested on the curve of her waist. "And after that there's... well, you know what comes after that."

The corner of Ryan's lips curved upwards in a smile. "I do, and I wouldn't mind getting to that point now. What do you think?"

"Nothing would make me happier than that."

"Then no more secrets from one another. *Ja?*"

This is what she had prayed for. This is what *Gott* intended. She felt deep within her soul that *Gott* would not have brought them together for any reason other than to be with one another. Throughout their spiritual journeys, they had helped each other along the way.

Matilda knew that she would have to tell him the truth if they didn't want secrets between them any longer.

She grabbed both his hands in her own and rubbed the back of his knuckles anxiously as she looked up at him with a shaky breath. "I have something to tell you. Something I've kept quiet for a long time."

He placed a finger on her lips. "Hush. Today isn't about secrets. Today is about *Gott*, about us, and our future."

"Are you saying that we have a future together?" She asked playfully, but her heart waited for his response.

Ryan rolled his eyes in humor and brushed back an errant strand of hair from her eyes. "Let's just say I've given it a lot thought and prayer as to where our relationship is going. I like the odds of us possibly joining some day."

Joy, the unfiltered kind of happiness, filled her entire being. It was the first time since Samuel's death that she felt something so purely. Unable to resist, she asked, "Joining in what?"

"Now *you're* being playful," he said, tugging on the string of her prayer *kapp*. "I meant courtship and then marriage. That is, if you want the same thing too."

He looked vulnerable for a brief moment before Matilda smiled broadly at him and stood on her tip toes to place a light kiss on his lips. She tasted fresh air and *kaffee* before pulling back with her hands gently resting on the muscles of his shoulders.

"Nothing would make me happier."

WANT MORE MATTIE AND RYAN?

Yes, the story of Matilda and Ryan continues in book #4, AN AMISH ENDING. It's been a year of testing for Ryan and a continuous trial for Mattie. Ryan has been baptized and there's real talk of courtship and marriage. Mattie still guards her secret. What happens when all is revealed? Will their love survive and will Mattie and Ryan finally marry? Be sure and sign up for the VIP mailing list so you'll know immediately when AN AMISH ENDING is released.

AN AMISH ENDING
www.AmishChristianRomance.com
Curious to learn more about Mattie's Rumspringa and how it ended? Read the short story BEYOND GOODBYE.

BEFORE GOODBYE
www.AmishChristianRomance.com

When Matilda Beachey is talked into going on Rumspringa with her best friend, she has no plans other than to return home to her Amish life as soon as possible. Instead she goes from Matilda to Mattie and meets Ryan Myers, an attractive, sexy older boy who teaches her a lot more than the Englischers way of life. What will she do when it's time to return home to her life and to the best friend who patiently waits for her return?

Missed reading the earlier book? Read the excerpt that follows from AN AMISH DECISION.

EXCERPT FROM *AN AMISH DECISION*

Matilda stood behind the table with her hands folded neatly in front of her as Englischers passed by, and she returned their smiling friendly greeting. She kept one eye carefully trained on her *kinner* who had long since grown bored of staying behind the table and were darting around to visit with other members of the community.

She watched as Rosella walked up to a tall Englischer man with similar blonde locks as hers and began to chat with him, a smile curving up her lips. Matilda tensed slightly, inwardly scolding her daughter's confidence in talking to strangers. It was a trait she noticed from the first day Rosella learned to talk. Unlike her siblings or her parents, Rosella had more confidence in her abilities to talk to people. Most of the time she talked her *bruders* into doing her chores or talked her way out of punishment.

The only person immune to it anymore was Matilda.

She started forward to disengage Rosella from the Englischer, but Lily sidled up next to Rosella and placed a protective arm around her niece's shoulders. Matilda let out a relieved breath and went to turn away when the man suddenly turned to look at whatever Lily was pointing to.

Her breath hitched within her throat at the sight of sapphire eyes, so much like Rosella's, and blonde hair slicked backwards to reveal a sharp face. A flash of heat curled at the base of her spine, and she stumbled into the table, stomach tightening into a million knots of dread. It couldn't be possible, no, it wasn't possible. The Englischer only dressed and looked like Ryan from his strong figure dressed casually in a pair of jeans and a white tee-shirt. Besides, he had no idea she lived in Monte Vista now since the last time they had seen each other she still lived in Lancaster and was only visiting Denver with her best friend Lucy.

"Matilda, are you all right?"

Rebecca was at her side in an instant, sweeping a fretting hand across the curve of her cheek to feel the heat there. Waving her *maemm's* concern away, Matilda forced an assuring smile on her face.

"*Ja*, Mama. I'm fine. It's probably just the heat."

Her *maemm* didn't let it go. Rebecca grabbed the metal box filled with their earnings and pulled out a ten dollar bill. "Here," she said, sliding it into Matilda's sweaty palm, "Take this and buy yourself a bottled water from the general store down the road. Take Lily with you to make sure you don't faint."

Matilda paled further at the thought of interrupting Lily's conversation with the handsome Englischer that looked so eerily like Ryan.

"That's okay, *maemm*. I can do it myself. Lily's busy."

Rebecca's eyes focused somewhere over her shoulder and a frown marred her features. "Nee she isn't."

Risking a glance over her shoulder, she let out a relieved breath to see that Lily now stood alone with Rosella. When she turned back around Rebecca's eyes were studying her intently. It was the same gaze that all Rebecca's *kinner* were familiar with; the one that said, "I know you are up to something and I will find out." Even as a fully grown woman she still shrunk back from it and hurried towards Lily.

"Rosella, can you please go to the tent with your *grohs-mammi*? Lily and I have to go to the store."

Lily frowned at her. "We do?"

"Just do it, please." Matilda snapped without meaning to. At Rosella's eyes widening, she back-peddled hastily. "I mean, *ja*. We have to go to the store. I'm feeling a bit faint. I'll get you something from the store to share with your *bruders*, Rosella. It was the Snickers bar right?"

Rosella's face brightened at the prospect of having a candy bar. It was one of her favorite Englischer candies. She'd always had such a sweet tooth.

"The one with the caramel and peanuts?"

"*Ja*. That one."

"*Danka*, Mama."

When Matilda straightened, Lily had a suspicious look as she stared at her sister. Matilda tensed at the strange expression.

"What?"

"You just look really pale and panicked."

"It's the heat."

"Right, the heat."

The two sisters squeezed their way out of the Farmers Market and took a quiet street to the general store. Matilda fanned herself with her hand, willing her body and emotions to calm down from the dread and fear shooting through her.

All of her efforts to calm herself vanished, however, when Lily turned to look at her and asked in a causal tone, "So, how do you know the Englischer named Ryan?"

AN AMISH DECISION

Visit Juliet Rohmer's Amazon author page and FOLLOW.

See all her books.

ALSO BY JULIET ROHMER

CIVIL WAR BRIDES

Love Amish fiction? Then you will probably find stories about young women who, after the Civil War, found themselves in all sorts of life situations where finding a husband became almost impossible. Discover how they handled this new era and whether they found true love in their midst.

For more information, go to
www.AmishChristianRomance.com.

THE RECIPE

The Homemade Peanut Butter Cake

1/4 cup peanut butter, smooth
1 1/2 cup sugar, brown
1/4 cup margarine, smooth
1/2 cup water, warm
1 cup sour milk, thick
2 eggs
2 cups flour
1 tsp. baking soda
1 tsp. salt

Bake 350° — 25 - 30 minutes

Grease and flour two 9 inch layer pans (or one 9 x 13 pan).

In a large mixing bowl, combine all the ingredients and mix for several minutes.

Pour into pan(s) and bake. When finished, use frosting.

Frosting

2 tbsp peanut butter, smooth
2 tbsp. butter
1 cup sugar, powdered
1 cup chocolate chips

Take the chocolate chips and the peanut butter and melt in a pan over low heat.

Blend other ingredients into the mixture until everything is thick, creamy and easy to spread on a cool cake.

ABOUT THE AUTHOR

Juliet Rohmer spends her days writing, reading, and researching. While she's not Amish, she formed a deep attachment for the Amish during her early years in Pennsylvania and values their deeply spiritual lifestyle. She enjoys writing inspirational stories whether they happen today or in years past. Fascinated with the post-Civil War era and the rise of mail order brides, Juliet looks forward to sharing their stories told in new and fresh ways.

For updates about new releases, as well as exclusive promotions, be sure and sign up for her VIP mailing list at AmishChristianRomance.com.

Visit Juliet Rohmer's Amazon Author page and stop by her Facebook page.

Amazon.com/Author/julietrohmer

Amish Romance Christian Inspirational Romance --
Juliet Rohmer

ENJOYED THIS BOOK?

You've made it to the end of my book and I love it. Having a reader make it all the way through is a writer's dream for every story written. If you enjoyed the story, would you consider leaving an honest review? Reviews are a big help to all authors, including me. They also let others know how much you enjoyed the story. You can leave your review for me at the end of this book.

Your review would mean a great deal to me.

Thank you,

Juliet Rohmer

APPENDIX - GLOSSARY

Ach - Oh

Bruder - Brother

Bobli - Baby

Daed - Father

Danka - Thank you

Dat - Term used for grandfather.

Englischer - Anyone who is not English.

Fraa - Wife

Grossmammi - Term used for grandmother.

Gott - God

Gut - God

Haus - house

Ja - Yes

Kapp - Cap (prayer cap)

Kaffee - Coffee

Kinner - Children

Kins-kind - Grandchildren

Mam - Term for one's mother.

Mann - Man

Mansleit - Men Folk

Ordnung - The agreed upon rules for living.

Rumspringa - The running around years

Sveshtah - Sister